3.50

Y0-BCF-063

DATE DUE

THUNDER DAM

by ARTHUR CATHERALL

THUNDER DAM

ILLUSTRATED BY OMAR DAVIS

Criterion Books
New York

Contents

1   Night without sleep   7

2   Disaster !   24

3   A wild-cat idea   45

4   Martin wins –   61

5   – and Po Het strikes   70

6   A buddha in danger   80

7   Unexpected hitch   94

8   Win all – or lose all   105

9   The temple and buddha are lost !   119

10 The showdown   127

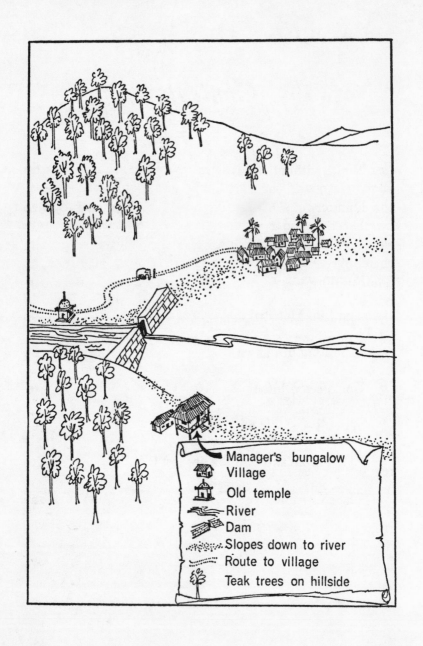

Manager's bungalow
Village
Old temple
River
Dam
Slopes down to river
Route to village
Teak trees on hillside

Night without sleep

For the first time in his life seventeen-year-old Martin Blake was getting ready to go to bed in a bamboo hut on the edge of the Burmese jungle. A little oil lamp burned on the camp table, and whenever he moved the light threw gigantic shadows on the walls and the nipa palm thatching above him. There was no ceiling in this room. The building was a simple affair of poles with woven bamboo walls. It had looked clean and cosy in daylight; but in the yellow light of the lamp it seemed to have developed an air of mystery – as if it belonged to some other world.

There came a creaking of bamboo from his father's room, and a few moments later George Blake came in. He was already in the voluminous pyjamas he wore when in the jungle; and they gave him an oddly Chinese appearance. Martin was beginning to smile when he realised two things: his father looked very serious, and he carried a revolver in his right hand.

'You had better take this,' he said, putting the weapon on the table, and laying by its side a small carton of cartridges. 'No, I'm not expecting an invasion, Martin. The head-hunters aren't out, or anything like that,' and for a moment a smile chased the serious expression away. He motioned his son to sit and made Martin's camp bed creak when he sat on the edge of it. In a quiet voice he went on :

'I have something to tell you. I had intended to be on the paddy-field when your plane landed, but I was held up. If I had managed to be there, I would have sent you back to Akyab until the trouble blew over.'

'Trouble?' Martin's heart began to beat a little faster. So that was why his father had seemed so strange during the evening meal. There had been little opportunity for private conversation until then, for after the tiny plane had landed on the bumpy paddy field Martin had to be introduced to the village headman; then he had been escorted to the tiny village to drink a ceremonial cup of coconut juice.

Time had seemed to fly, and when he walked over to the 'bungalow', a three-bedroomed bamboo hut, the sun had set and it was time to have a bath, change into clean clothes and sit down to the last meal of the day.

To Martin's surprise his father had not seemed himself. Normally he would have been asking questions about the family back home, and perhaps cracking jokes – for he had a fund of funny stories for any and every occasion. But he had said little, sitting rather pre-occupied during the meal.

Now, when they were both ready for bed, his father broke the ice, hinting at trouble.

'Is it serious?' Martin went on, when his father seemed to have forgotten what he came in for, and was staring into space, his eyes puckered in a frown. 'What kind of trouble?'

'You have always got to have an eye cocked for trouble when you are working teak forests,' his father said at last, nipping off the end of a Burma cheroot and flicking his lighter to life. 'That is why I brought you out while you were still in your teens. If you can grow up with these people you understand them all the better. And you have a lot to learn, Martin. It isn't just a matter of supervising the felling of timber. You have to be a doctor to humans, a veterinary surgeon to the elephants, a weather forecaster, a high court judge, the lot. At times you have got to be able to cast out devils. That is what we are up against at the moment.'

'Devils!' and Martin began to smile, but his smile faded at the serious expression on his father's face.

'You know, Martin, I have been a *teak wallah* ever since the end of the war with Japan,' his father said soberly. 'First I worked for the teak company, then when it was nationalized I worked for the Burmese Government. Three years ago I got a concession to work the teak in this valley. I have put every penny we have into it, for you can't just cut teak and ship it out. First the trees have to be ringed, to kill them. After that they must be left standing for a couple of years while they dry out, otherwise they won't float downstream.'

He puffed at his cigar for a moment or so as if collecting his thoughts, then went on:

'Nobody ever made a success of working the teak in this valley. You see, there was never enough water coming down at any one time to float the logs out. That's why I got the concession. It meant building a dam.'

'Well, that is built, isn't it?' Martin suggested.

'Oh, it's built right enough,' his father agreed, 'and I

thought I had got over another major snag. In the valley there is a small, very old Burmese temple. Who built it I don't know, but as usual there was a brass buddha in it. When I brought my *oozies* (elephant men) and their families here, they adopted the temple, took a lamp up to it, and laid their offerings before the buddha.'

'But they must have known you were going to flood the valley,' Martin murmured.

'Not at first. Building a dam to get water isn't usual. Anyway, I told them and I suggested to the headman, Po Het, that I would build another temple nearer the village. That seemed to be a good idea, and there were no objections. For convenience we built the temple at the end of the village street. The buddha was moved, and everything seemed fine. Then, two days ago, the buddha vanished.'

'Vanished! You mean somebody stole it?'

'No! It wasn't stolen. Somebody just transferred it to the old temple. They fixed up the little lamp and the temple ornaments,' George Blake said grimly. 'I personally saw to it that it was carried back. I discussed the matter with Po Het, and we laid a trap. It was a simple trigger and gong effort, so that if anybody entered the temple after nightfall, the gong would sound, and the villagers would be able to rush out and catch the idiots who were playing this silly game. Well, it didn't work!'

'You mean . . .'

'Yes, the buddha was moved again. Somebody knew about the trap, disconnected the string, and carted the brass buddha back to the old temple again. They took the lamp and the temple ornaments – no easy thing for that buddha weighs at least two hundredweights. So it wasn't a one-man show.'

'It seems crazy to me,' Martin said frowning. 'What was the idea?'

'Well, you have to understand the way these jungle people think to see what lay behind this,' his father said quietly. 'When I said earlier that there were times when I had to be able to deal with devils I wasn't joking. Jungle people believe in spirits – *nats* they call them. I'll give you an example: whenever an elephant man is killed – and the big tuskers sometimes turn killer when they are on *musth* – '

'*Musth*? Is that when the treacly stuff starts coming out of little orifices above the eyes and the tuskers become vicious?' Martin asked, and his father nodded.

'Yes, it comes on periodically, and then the elephant has to be chained up. Anyway, what I was telling you was that if an elephant kills its *oozie* I have to sign a note – from me to the jungle spirits, and give it to the wife . . . that note says the *oozie* is released from service with me and can be admitted to the hereafter, and live with the jungle *nats*.'

Martin stared at his father, and felt a little chill creep up his spine. This was something he had not known, though with his father's help, through weekly tape recordings and letters, he had been studying teak work and the Burmese language for the past four years.

'The trouble is that the villagers are now frightened. They think that the *nats* don't like the idea of the buddha being taken away from his old temple. Po Het hasn't said

anything definite to me about it, but I know what the
men are talking about. They are getting to the point where
they could go on strike if I insist on flooding the valley.
They are going to ask me to allow the buddha to remain
in the old temple.'

'But you can't do that!'

'No,' his father shook his head slowly. 'I can't. If I don't
have plenty of water I can't float my logs down. That is
what is worrying me. Time is short, and the monsoon will
begin any day now – the valley will be flooded and the
temple will be under water. I have got to think of something. The people won't stand for the flooding of their
temple, and I don't blame them. We wouldn't like one of
our churches to be damaged.'

He flicked the ash from the end of his cheroot, then
shrugged and smiled.

'You're not to worry, Martin. You come up against
all kinds of troubles, and you get by. Anyway, about this
revolver. I got it for you, though I didn't intend to hand it
over just yet. They are not playthings. Most jungle wal-
lahs keep one under their pillow at night. There are wild
animals in the jungle – the odd tiger has been known to
visit a camp. When they get old, or maybe lamed with a
sliver of bamboo through a paw and cannot hunt, they
sometimes turn man-eater. Panthers, too, prowl around,
especially if you keep a dog. I stopped keeping pets years
ago for that reason.'

'But you aren't giving me the revolver now because of
those things,' Martin suggested. His father looked at him
for a moment then shook his head.

'No, I'm not,' he agreed. 'I'm giving it to you because I think there is someone trying to stop me getting out my teak. Someone who realises that if I can be stopped – there is a fortune waiting for whoever follows me. If they can drive me out they can use the dam and get the teak. And you know, Martin, we have got to get the logs out this season. If we don't manage it – we are broke. We haven't the cash to hang on for another year.'

He picked up the revolver and broke it. Opening the carton of cartridges he loaded the chambers, snapped the gun shut, pushed the safety catch on then pointing the weapon at the floor, tried to pull the trigger.

'That is something you have always got to bear in mind, Martin. Keep your revolver loaded, but keep the safety catch on. As long as the catch is on, there is no chance of an accident. Now, unload it and load it again.' He pushed the Smith and Wesson across to his son.

Martin took the weapon rather gingerly. He had seen his share of cowboy films on television where rangy cowpunchers, or sheriffs, or villains, 'reached' for a gun and 'fanned' the trigger as they sprayed lead at their enemies. It was rather different when you had a real weapon in your hands.

Watched by his father he broke the revolver and took out the cartridges. He closed the gun again, spun the barrel to make sure there were no shells left, then pointing the muzzle downwards he squeezed the trigger. There was a sharp click, which was repeated each time he squeezed the trigger. He pushed the safety catch to the 'on' position, and now there was no click when he tried to fire.

'I'm not suggesting you should try and shoot anybody if trouble comes,' his father said when Martin was pushing cartridges into the gun again. 'It is surprising what effect a shot has when it is fired into the air or into the ground.'

He rose, stubbed his cheroot into a beautifully hammered copper ash tray then rose.

'Don't worry too much,' and he clapped a hand on Martin's shoulder. 'The chap who gets by in this country is the one who is prepared. You know what we are up against. Get to sleep as soon as you can. We'll be up early, for I want to take you round the valley and show you the dam. I'm rather proud of it. Never done dam building before – but it's a good job, even though I'm not the one who should say that. Good night!'

'Good night, Father,' and Martin stood gazing after his father until the rickety door was pulled shut. He heard the creak of bamboo as his father walked the yard or so along the veranda to his own room; then he lifted his pillow and laid the revolver there.

There was a sudden hiss from his little oil lamp, and the flame flickered for a moment. In the second or so that the door had been open some insect had come in and making straight for the lamp had committed suicide in its flame. It reminded Martin about the mosquitos, and he hurriedly undressed, lifted the mosquito netting and crawled into bed.

When he pushed a hand under the netting to turn out the light it seemed to be a 'go-ahead' signal to the invisible army of winged pests. His father was already in bed, so there was no sound at all from the next room, even though only a thin wall of woven bamboo divided father and son. Lying there in the darkness Martin was aware almost at once of the thin high whine of mosquitos.

He could almost tell when they struck the netting which safeguarded him. The high pitched whine would stop for a second, then begin again. From the small clump of trees behind their bamboo home came a never ending chatter – like the rustling of countless beans against one another. That sound was made by the cicadas, a beetle-like insect with which the branches seemed to be crowded.

Then, and it made his heart miss a beat, something in the room itself began calling. It was a quick 'tuktoo . . . tuktoo . . . tuktoo . . . tuktoo' going on for perhaps twenty seconds, but with the interval between the calls growing greater. The calls ended with a tired little 'augh!' as if the mosquito-hunting 'tuktoo' lizard had decided it was time to go to sleep.

Martin punched a depression in his pillow and wriggled into a more comfortable position on his camp bed. He was tired, for his journey out to Burma from Britain had been almost non-stop. From home by luxurious high-flying jet to Calcutta; then by turbo-prop from Calcutta to Akyab Island on the north Burma coast, and by a rickety little Auster aircraft inland to this jungle-clad country where his father had his camp.

The tuktoo lizard began calling again, stopped, started again, and seemed as if it would go on for ever, despite the tired little 'aughs' at the end of his stacatto 'tuktoo' calls.

Martin drew the bedsheet above his ears in the hope of cutting off the sounds, but was soon throwing the sheet back. The heat was stifling. After months of dry, baking heat, the monsoon clouds were gathe.ing and the air was heavy with humidity. Martin began to count in the hope that he would drift off to sleep despite the whining of the mosquitos and the constant 'tuktoo' calls from the lizard on the bamboo wall.

He must have drifted into a doze, but came back to consciousness at the cry of an owl somewhere in the trees. The fright sent gooseflesh creeping up his cheeks, and he wiped a damp hand across his forehead. Being a *'teakwallah'*, as his father was, had always seemed a romantic and exciting way of earning a living. He had never thought about this side of the life.

Then, as he turned restlessly over, he saw a patch of moonlight on the floor. It was a long silver rectangle, the light coming in through a broken slat in the bamboo curtain. He stared at it for a moment, and was about to close his eyes when a shadow moved into the silvery light.

Any thought of sleep was banished at once when he realised that the visitor was a rat. His father had warned him that he might hear the 'tree rats' playing about in the nipa-palm thatching of the building. Now, to his disgust, as his eyes focused better, he saw that the rat had what looked like a piece of chocolate.

It was trying to bite off the silver foil wrapping, and Martin suddenly remembered that he had left a small block of chocolate in his bush jacket pocket. The idea that a rat had actually been in his pocket filled him with horror and he was on the point of leaping out of bed when he remembered that he would first have to untuck the mosquito netting.

'And by the time I do that the dirty little thief will be gone,' he thought, and sank back again on the pillow. He could hear the rat nibbling and clawing at the silver foil. Then every sound ceased. He lifted his head. The rat was still there, but now it was looking towards the door.

It had heard something; some sound too slight for Martin's ears. Seconds passed and then the rat was gone. The piece of chocolate was dropped, there was a faint scratching on the bamboo wall, then silence. In the heavy, breathless silence, Martin heard laboured breathing; not from his father's bedroom, but from somewhere outside.

His heart began to thump. All the things his father had spoken of just before they went to bed flashed through his mind. The *nats* (spirits); the idea that someone was trying to ruin them; and the fact that it was serious enough for his father to arm him with a revolver.

At that thought Martin slipped a hand under the pillow. The revolver was warm, and he could not remember, now, whether he had left the safety catch on or off. Nor could he remember which way to move it. A moment later he heard the faint creak of the veranda floor as someone stepped on to the bamboo laths.

Then, without warning, a gun bellowed. To Martin, whose nerves were stretched to breaking point, it sounded like a clap of thunder. It had been fired in the next room, his father's room, for the flash lit up every crack and split in the plaited bamboo wall.

Martin tried to hurl himself out of bed, the gun in his right hand; but he had forgotten the fine-meshed mosquito netting tucked securely under his mattress. Like a salmon in a landing net, he lurched forward and a moment later fell on the floor with the bed on top of him.

As he hit the floor he heard a man shriek, his voice filled with terror:

'*Thakin ... Thakin* Blake ... don't shoot. It is me, Po Het.'

A few seconds later there came the thump of feet hitting the floor in the next room, then George Blake shouted:

'Martin, are you all right? What's happened?'

Martin tried to answer, but he was struggling with the mosquito net, and with the camp bed turned over on top of him, was not having much success in disentangling himself. He was just turning the bed off him when the door burst open and the light of a torch lit up the room.

When Martin scrambled to his feet he faced his father. George Blake had a smoking revolver in one hand, a torch in the other, while behind him, his eyes round with fear, stood the village headman.

'You O.K?' George demanded, and when Martin nodded, too breathless and shaken to speak, his father turned to the Burmese headman. His voice was cold with repressed anger as he asked: 'Po Het, what were you doing on my veranda at this time of night? Only *dacoits* (thieves) and murderers creep about at night. Have you not already learned that no one can creep up to my bungalow unheard? You are fortunate I did not shoot you dead.'

'Yes, *thakin*,' Po Het agreed, and he was trembling. 'I would have shouted but I was afraid of the *nats*. I did not want them to know that I came to warn you and give you the bad news.'

'Bad news! What are you talking about? What has happened?'

'The temple, *thakin*,' the headman faltered. 'The *nats* have visited it again. Come to the door and look. A woman woke to attend to a fretful child and saw the glow. She gave the alarm.'

They hurried on to the veranda and even in the moonlight it was easy to see that a fire was raging somewhere in the little village.

Martin and his father dressed as quickly as possible and followed Po Het across the dried-up paddy fields. The glow was fading now, and when they got to the little street of bamboo huts there were only a few smouldering struts of wood left of the new temple.

The villagers were standing in little frightened groups, and they stared goggle-eyed at the two Englishmen as they hurried past. Martin heard his father grunt, then he turned to the headman and asked:

'Who has moved the lamp? The temple lamp?'

Po Het could only gulp and shake his head.

'The buddha has been moved again,' George Blake said in an aside to Martin. Then to the headman he snapped: 'Every man must get a torch. We will go up and see if the buddha is back in his old home.'

In a matter of minutes a line of men carrying torches moved up the valley. Each man kept as close as possible to his neighbour, and all of them were cold with fear – fear that the jungle *nats* might suddenly strike at them from the sombre gloom of the trees.

They crossed the southern end of the dam, and now the red light of the torches was reflected in the water which was already collecting in the upper part of the valley. It was an eerie scene, and though Martin did not believe in ghosts or *nats,* he kept having unaccountable icy chills striking down his back.

When they reached the old temple there was a faint musical tinkling coming from the many tinsel ornaments bedecking the eaves, for here a light breeze was blowing. Martin followed his father to the open front of the tiny temple. Just inside a lamp burned, and shone on the paunchy figure of the buddha. The brass figure seemed to be smiling serenely at the two Britishers.

'Just as before,' Martin's father said bitterly. 'They brought the buddha here, the lamp, and even the temple ornaments. There must be at least half a dozen men involved in this.'

'Village men?' Martin asked, and got only an angry shrug from his father.

'Go back to your sleep, and let no man worry,' Martin's father said, and laying a hand on Po Het's shoulder held him there until the line of torch-bearing Burmese were on their way, then he said: 'There will be no work on the logs tomorrow, Po Het. The elephants will be paraded as usual – but no man is to move down the valley.'

'What is this, then, *thakin* Blake?' Po Het asked. 'Are you stopping all work?'

'Oh, no! I still intend to flood the valley when the rains come – but first of all I am going to make a peace offering to the *nats*. They seem to dislike the idea of having the buddha in the temple I built for them. So . . . we will leave the buddha where he is.'

'But if the valley is flooded, *thakin,* the temple will drown!' Po Het protested.

'No, I would not let that happen, Po Het. Tomorrow I am going to build a raft of logs under the temple . . . and haul it further up the hillside, beyond where the waters can reach it. That ought to pacify the *nats,* and anyone else interested in keeping the buddha in his old resting place.'

Po Het looked startled, but made no comment. He walked in silence back to the village, where the men were already dispersing to their huts. Martin and his father returned to their bungalow, where they made a cup of tea before going back to bed.

By this time the headman was also in bed, but not to sleep. He lay for half an hour until he was sure that his wife was sound asleep, then he rose. From the back room he took a small lamp and a pot of honey. The moon was now dropping down towards the hill tops, and soon everything would be dark. There was no sound from the other huts and Po Het slipped behind his hut and moved across to the clearing where the elephants were assembled each morning. Here the harnesses hung from low branches, out of reach of rats and ants.

Po Het searched among the hanging harnesses until he found the two sets belonging to the biggest tuskers. When logs proved too heavy to be hauled by a single tusker, a team would be harnessed in line and one of the biggest elephants put in the lead. He selected the breast bands of the two lead elephants, and smeared the inside of the broad woven bands with honey. Then he soaked two pieces of string in honey, tied one to each harness band and let it trail down to the ground.

Smearing the fluffed-out end of a piece of rope with honey he dragged this across the sun-baked clearing to where the bushes and undergrowth began. There the jungle floor was carpeted thick with dead leaves – the home of millions of ants. He re-soaked his piece of rope and stroked the end across the ground in a dozen different lines, all leading back to the trail he had laid across the clearing.

Then filling his pipe he sat back and smoked, his lamp turned down to no more than a tiny glimmer. When he finished his first pipe he turned the lamp higher and studied the unseen honey tracks. They were clearly visible now as inch wide black lines, which on closer inspection were revealed as thousands of scurrying ants, all following the honey trail.

Po Het smoked two more pipes of tobacco before rising to examine the harness. When he looked at the breast bands they were a seething black mass of ants. The strings leading from the ground were also thick with the hungry insects – ants going up and ants returning. The headman brushed the ants off one harness band so that he could examine the material.

A smile creased his dark face as he saw that hundreds

of pincer-like jaws had done all he hoped for and seriously weakened the bands. Then he spent ten minutes brushing ants off and stamping on thousands waiting their turn to climb the strings. Before he returned to his hut there was no obvious sight of what had happened. He had smoothed out the back of the harness so that a casual glance would not reveal the damage that had been done. Then he went to bed.

2

Disaster !

Martin was wakened by his father's Burmese cook lifting the mosquito net and offering him a cup of tea. The sun was up and he could hear his father moving about. Outside the yellow and black minah birds were whistling cheekily as they foraged for scraps about the bungalow kitchen. As yet the air was no more than pleasantly warm and the brilliantly blue sky promised another glorious day.

Forty minutes later he and his father were moving up the valley, towards the dam. The nature of this valley had already defeated Burmese teak men, for it was narrow and steep sided at its head, then widened out very rapidly. The sides of the hills were rich in good teak, but no one had yet been able to get the logs away.

Burma is a wild country, with few roads and fewer railways. The one economical method of moving teak is by floating it down the rivers. The logs are cut and stacked by the side of the dried-up river beds. Then, when the monsoon storms break over the hills the dry river beds are transformed for a few hours into howling torrents.

Teams of elephants work along the river banks, release logs which jam and keep the teak moving. It worked well in many valleys, but it had not worked in this. This valley widened out too quickly, thus allowing the monsoon floods to spread out and lose their power. That was the reason for the failure of earlier efforts; and the main reason why George Blake had been granted the teak concession.

When they stood on the dam he said:

'I had to build this so I could gather a terrific weight of water. I've built the sluice gate big, so that when I open it there'll be a mighty rush which will sweep all our timber down to the main stream. If we can do that . . . we are all right. If we can't – we're broke. It is as simple as that, for I've sunk every penny I have in this venture.'

Martin stood on the top of the dam and looked about him. The sluice gate was of teak, and was worked by what looked like capstans, with bars as in the old-time sailing ships. Half a dozen men on each capstan* could open the gate. The little stream which never dried up had been dammed for some weeks now, and had formed a small lake in the upper part of the valley.

For one man to do work like this, with only the help of unskilled Burmese and a dozen elephants was a mighty achievement, and Martin realised more than ever that his father was not only a skilled engineer, but a man with boundless courage and resourcefulness. If he won it would be a triumph of courage and ingenuity over amazing odds.

The sound of voices made them look to the right, and they saw the elephants moving along the narrow track some ten feet above the present water level. One man rode each beast and one walked by its head.

'The boy at the elephant's head is the *pajaik*, or assistant,' Martin's father explained. 'He hooks on the drag

---

* Revolving barrel, worked by men walking round and pushing horizontal levers, for winding cable in.

chains to the logs, and he has to go out each morning to find the elephant.'

'To find it?' Martin queried.

'There are no stables for our elephants,' his father chuckled. 'Each evening the *oozie* turns his beast free – well, its hind legs are shackled – but even so they often wander miles away looking for fodder. You know an elephant will eat as much as 600 pounds of stuff every day. The *oozie* checks his harness when his elephant has gone off, but it is the responsibility of the *pajaik* to bring the beast back in the morning. If you had been born a Burmese instead of an Englishman, young fellow, you would know what real work was. These boys sometimes walk eight or nine miles in a morning before they eat.'

Martin stared; he was learning quickly, and when they moved across to the side of the valley where the elephants were gathered near the old temple, he looked at the *pajaiks* with interest and respect. They seemed to be about his own age, slim, clean limbed youths of between sixteen and eighteen years.

Though Martin did not know it, his father had been across to the village at sunrise, and given orders for spades and planks, hammers and six-inch nails as well as stout ropes to be brought along.

For the next few hours there was tremendous activity about the temple. It was a small building, about sixteen feet square, and made from teak. With the help of two elephants, the temple was slightly tilted to enable planks to be inserted under the floor, and an hour after noon a platform had been built under the temple.

Then dragging chains were fastened in place and the twelve elephants hooked together in two lines of six. The plan was simple enough. With care they ought to be able to drag the temple along the track and up to a height where not even the greatest flood could reach it.

Martin's father raised a handkerchief, and when he was sure all the *oozies* were watching him, he swept the handkerchief down as a signal for the dragging to begin.

'Yoo . . . yoo . . . yoo!' All twelve *oozies* took up the chant at once. 'Yoo...yoo...yoo (pull, pull, pull!)!' The great beasts, all of them tuskers, leaned slowly forward into their harness, the chains linking them together tightened, and with a grunt and a sudden crunching of earth, the temple on its platform began to move up the slope.

Martin's heart was thumping with excitement and pride. Pride that his father could organise a thing like this, for though the temple was quite small it must have been heavy, and it had been a skilful piece of work raising it on to the crude platform.

Then, without warning, there was a sudden pistol-like *crack*. Martin turned and was in time to see two things happening in the same instant. The breast band of the leading elephant had parted. It came winging back like a giant whip, at the same moment the elephant staggered forward, and his tusks dug some eight inches into the ground.

In a matter of seconds there was pandemonium. The chain and the broken harness slapped the elephant behind across the head, just as the *oozie*, seeing the danger, leaped for his life. Almost at once there was a second crack, and the harness of the other leading elephant broke.

Martin watched the *oozie* who had jumped to escape injury, and was starting to run to the man's aid even before he vanished under the surface of the water below. The track along which the temple was to be dragged, had been worn into the hillside by countless generations of feet. It rose steeply to the hill side, and dropped just as steeply to the water.

The *oozie* touched the bank once with his heels, and then threw up a wave of water and brown mud as he went down and out of sight. Martin slithered down the bank, ready to give the man a hand when he came to the surface . . . but he did not reappear !

On the track above there were roars and squeals from the elephants, mingled with confused shouts from the *oozies* as they struggled to calm their panicking tuskers. The one which had been struck by the swinging chain was roaring, in pain and anger, his panic-stricken moves threatening to tumble the elephant behind him down the bank into the water.

George Blake was shouting and in the thick of the chaotic struggle. Martin whipped off his bush jacket, stared intently at the muddy water for a moment, then slid in. Something had happened to the *oozie,* and if he was not got out now he would not be got out alive.

Only when he began to tread water did Martin realise why the man had not come up. Below the surface there was nothing but semi-liquid mud. He could feel it about his feet, thick, porridgy stuff. If he had stopped to think he would not have swum below the surface. There was the threat of a horrible choking death awaiting anyone trapped in that stuff, for the mud was cumbered with dead weeds, wiry-like stalks which had been withered by the sun until the valley began to fill up with water.

A feebly moving arm swept across Martin's face as he stroked downwards. The man below was fighting for his life, fighting feebly, and probably almost unconscious. Martin grabbed the arm and kicked mightily. By the time his head broke surface his lungs felt as if they were on fire, and he had red spots floating before his eyes.

Somehow he got the Burman's face above the surface, and held him there while he filled and re-filled his lungs. Then he turned towards the bank, sure that there would be a dozen pairs of willing hands anxious to help him out.

There was no one there. He could see frightened and angry elephants crowding one another; the *oozies,* with almost unbelievable courage, were still sticking to their seats on the necks of their mounts, and fighting for control.

'Help! Help!' His cry for aid could hardly have been heard in the bedlam of noise, yet suddenly a *pajaik* slid down the bank. He was a slim, young man, his skin light copper in colour; and his eyes were wide with fear when he saw what Martin was supporting above the level of the churned up mud and water.

The thin arms proved to be much stronger than they looked, and with the *pajaik's* help the limp form was hauled up the bank. Then the boy helped Martin out of the water, and between them they carried the *oozie* down the track and to the lower side of the temple.

'Is he dead, *thakin*?' and there was terror in the boy's voice.

Martin could only reply with a headshake. He did not know, and at the moment he had no breath for words. He turned the limp form face down, head to one side. With trembling fingers he cleared the mouth of mud and weed while the young Burmese watched him, hands clasped in an attitude of entreaty.

Forgetting the hub-bub on the track beyond the temple, Martin began to give the *oozie* artificial respiration. He was covered with mud, and panting; yet somehow he managed to keep on. The noise further up the track began to subside, and finally there was only one elephant squealing – the tusker who had taken the full force of the draw chain when it swung back.

From what seemed a great distance Martin heard a man shout:

'He is there, behind the temple,' and a minute later someone ran to him and laying a hand on his shoulder said urgently:

'*Thakin, thakin* ... please come. Your father is hurt ... dead, I think!'

At the same moment the unconscious man coughed, cleared a piece of weed and mud from his throat, and drew a deep, sighing breath. Martin knelt there, still automatically carrying on with the work of bringing the half-drowned man back to life. It took a few seconds for the message to sink into his sub-consciousness. His father was dead! He couldn't be! It was only a matter of minutes since he had been in the thick of the battle, encouraging the *oozies* and trying to quell the panic among the elephants.

Yet the Burmese who had brought the news was insistent, shaking Martin by the shoulder as he said once more:

'*Thakin*, your father has been struck by one of the elephants. He is lying on the ground – very still.'

Perhaps it was the last phrase 'very still' which did the trick. Martin went suddenly quite cold with horror. It was like a bad dream, except that he knew he was not dreaming. Then the *pajaik* who had helped him get the *oozie* out of the mud and who had dropped to one knee by Martin's side, clasped the young Britisher by the left arm and his eyes were wide with terror when he said:

'*Thakin* – will my father live? Make him live! Please make him live.'

That broke the icy spell which had gripped Martin's mind like a clamp. He half rose, and tried to look past the front of the temple to where the elephants and the *oozies* were still milling around. As he did so the young *pajaik* clutched him in an even fiercer grip, crying:

'*Thakin*, do not leave my father now. Bring him back to life. Only you can bring him back to life.'

Just for a split second Martin tensed, ready to fling the boy's grip off his arm. Then he checked the impulse and re-kneeling, carried on with the resuscitation. It was perhaps the hardest moment of his life, for he put aside the desire to go and see what had happened to his own father, to make sure this youngster's father lived.

Another five minutes saw a marked change in the man

on the ground. He regained consciousness and even tried
to lever himself up. He was feeling very sick, and gulping
air laboriously, but he was breathing automatically, and
would live. His son was talking to him, telling him he
would be all right very soon, and his crisis was over.

Martin got to his feet, suddenly conscious that a dozen
men and youths were staring at him. As he walked up the
track, and past the temple, the little group of Burmese followed him, ominously silent.

The elephants had been brought under control again,
while the one which had been injured was being led back
to the village. An *oozie* was riding him, a *pajaik* was walking alongside him, the point of a spear on a level with the
beast's right eye; it was a silent reminder that he must be-
have himself. Blood was coming from a gash where the
chain had struck him, and he was making a queer grumb-
ling sound as he plodded away.

Martin pushed through the ring of men who stood staring at George Blake. The Britisher was lying in a queerly
twisted position, and Martin stopped, afraid to go on. The
ring of Burmese widened slowly, the men and youths
drawing back as if they did not wish to intrude on Martin's grief.

Then Po Het, the headman, came across. He made a
little sign of obeisance and murmured:

'It was an accident, *thakin*. Your father was trying to
calm a tusker who had been jabbed by another. Then the
big bull we call Jade Eyes swung round as the tusker who
was hurt by the chain reared up. It happened in the wink
of an eye. An elephant's tusk is a powerful weapon,

thakin, and your father's legs were just swept from under him.' Then, as an afterthought, he added: 'Perhaps he is not dead, yet.'

Afraid, yet conscious that all eyes were on him, Martin moved forward and dropped to one knee. Gently he turned his father's face so that it was not against the hard brick ground, and as he did so the 'dead' man spoke. It was a blurred sort of whisper, half plea, half command:

'Don't . . . don't move me yet.' That George Blake was still badly dazed was evident from the fact that he spoke in Burmese, not realising that it was his son who was kneeling by his side.

For Martin it was a moment when he did not know whether to laugh or cry. The relief was so great that he had an urge to jump to his feet; and yet his eyes filled with unaccustomed tears. That his father should be lying there, limp, and not himself, was a shock which left him trembling.

The first thing which came to his mind was a doctor. They must get a doctor. He turned to look for Po Het, and the headman came forward.

'A doctor; we must have a doctor,' Martin said breathlessly. 'How soon can we get one?'

Po Het's face clouded over. He shook his head slowly. There were no doctors in jungle country. Their doctor had been the man lying on the ground. If anyone was sick or hurt, it was *thakin* Blake who was doctor and surgeon.

'But we must be able to get a doctor from somewhere,' Martin insisted, a new fear choking him. 'My father must have a doctor. Surely there . . . '

'Martin!' George Blake's head was clearing and though it cost him an effort and the pain brought a dew of perspiration to his forehead, he half turned so that he could look up at his son.

'Father, are you badly hurt? What can I do? Where is the nearest doctor?'

Somehow his father managed a wan smile. He lifted a dust covered hand to tap his own chest.

'I'm the doctor round here, Martin,' he said slowly. 'And don't panic. That is the last thing you can afford to do out here,' and as Martin stared at him, silent and horrified, George Blake went on: 'Worse things than this happen, my boy. And I'm not going to die. Just simmer down. Am I bleeding anywhere?'

That gave Martin a stab in the heart. It was something he had not noticed, but a careful inspection of his father revealed no outward wound. The legs looked odd, and he said so. His father nodded.

'Broken, I expect,' he said. 'Old Jade Eyes swiped me pretty hard, and I can remember being pitched into the air. Send for my campbed, and blankets. Where's Po Het?'

The headman came forward, and George Blake, still lying flat in the dust, his sun bronzed face showing just a hint of greyness about the mouth, gave Po Het instructions. He was to send two of his most experienced men west to a small town where there was a telephone. From there a telephone message was to be sent to Akyab, asking for a doctor to be sent out by plane. The message was to contain the news that the injured man was George Blake, and there were probably broken legs to be set.

'Will the doctor get here today?' Martin asked.

'Today!' George Blake shook his head. 'Martin, you are not at home now. The men might get to where the telephone is by tomorrow evening, if they are lucky.'

Martin closed his eyes and winced at the thought. It seemed as if his whole world had suddenly crumpled to bits. He would have gone to pieces but for his father. Though in pain, George Blake preserved a quiet calm which soothed the nerves of everyone.

When the *oozies* arrived with the camp bed and the blankets George Blake gave Martin instructions on putting temporary splints on the broken legs. They were padded with blankets, and then the injured man was lifted gently on to the camp bed. There was no talking, and no man could have been handled with greater care. Then the bed was lifted and the procession made its way along the track, past the end of the dam, and finally across the rough ground to the bungalow.

Martin's father told the headman to take his men back to the village for the day and when they were gone he instructed the cook to bring in some length of broad bamboo. Then, as if he were asking the simplest of things he said:

'Martin, you've got to splint my legs properly now. It may be three or four days before a doctor gets here. I shall have to try to lie still, but I must have them well splinted so that if I do move I can't do any more damage.'

Wrapping the broken legs in blanketing had been bad enough; splinting them properly was a nerve wracking

ordeal, and Martin was wet with perspiration by the time
he had finished. His father, propped up by pillows and
blankets, smoked a cheroot, watching and giving instructions. He gave no sign that he was in pain, but his face
was dappled with beads of perspiration when Martin tied
the final knot. He blew out a great sigh of relief when the
work was done and somehow managed a nod and an encouraging smile.

'First class, Martin,' he said, and clapping his hands for
the cook, instructed the man to bring in the lunch. 'Now
don't say you aren't hungry,' he chaffed. 'I know how you
feel, and I'm proud of you. I know how I felt the first
time I had to handle a casualty. If you are going to be a
teak-wallah you have to face up to all sorts of things – and
you have made a very good start.'

With the back of one hand he wiped the perspiration
from his forehead, stubbed the butt of his cheroot in an
ash tray, and winked at his son.

'In some apprenticeships, Martin, you do little else at
first but make cups of tea for the workmen, or run
errands. In this apprenticeship you are going to jump
right in, feet first. I'm unlikely to be able to move from
here for sometime, so you are going to be promoted now.'

Martin blew out a long breath and mopped his face. He
was feeling spent, and yet deep inside knew a glow of
triumph. It might seem a small thing to have splinted two
broken legs. He had done splinting while a Boy Scout, but
it had only been pretence, for the patient's legs had not
been broken. In the Scout room it had been a game. What
he had just done was reality.

The cook brought in the midday meal, and not until they had finished and George Blake was smoking a cheroot did he mention the accident.

'There is one thing you will soon learn about the Burmese *oozie*. He is a light-hearted chap, Martin, and a great gambler. He will gamble his shirt away when they start playing cards; but he *never gambles with his work*. When the day ends he turns his elephant loose to find its fodder, and his first job then is to examine the harness. The breast band is the vital part. Dragging chains seldom break, but a breast band wears quickly, yet I have never known one break before today.'

'But *two* broke,' Martin pointed out. 'One after the other.'

'Yes,' his father agreed, 'and both on the leading elephants. As far as I am concerned it was more than a coincidence. Somebody planned it. The same person, or persons, who have been monkeying about with the buddha. The same people who set the new temple on fire. I don't know who it is. I don't think the *oozies* know. Some of them have worked with me for years, and I think one of them would have dropped me a hint if they had known.'

He puffed at his cheroot for a few moments while Martin waited anxiously. If what his father said was true, they were indeed in real trouble.

'It would have been hard going even if I had been fit,' his father went on at last. 'It is much worse now that I am having to leave it to you. You have got to be my eyes, my voice, and my hands, Martin. I wish you hadn't to do this – and especially as you have only just got here; but it is that, or go bankrupt. It's a tough job, I'm afraid.'

Martin was shocked, but said nothing.

'I can see what they want,' his father continued. 'It boils down to this: I have promised that getting out teak will not interfere with the people's religion. That means the buddha and the temple. I must flood the valley or I can't get the teak floated down to the main river. If I flood the valley then I must get the temple and the buddha higher up the valley side, where the water cannot reach them. You can imagine the fuss there would be if I left them where they are and then let the valley flood them.'

'Are there no police we could call in?' Martin asked.

'No!' his father shook his head soberly. 'What the villagers are saying is that *nats* are moving the buddha. You can't ask police to arrest a *nat*. In any case, it would take several days to get police here – and you saw the trees with the red flowers.'

Martin nodded. His father had explained the significance of the flame-of-the-forest trees. They bloomed three times during the hot season. At the third blooming one could expect the rains to come within a day, two days at the most. Just now the trees were laden with the lovely red flowers – and it was for the third time this season.

'Well, here are your first orders, Martin,' George Blake said. 'Go to the village and get hold of Po Het. Tell him I say he is to muster the *oozies* and their elephants. All breast bands are to be examined, and then they are to go back to the temple and haul it higher up the track. If we can get it a dozen feet higher it will be clear of the flood water.'

As Martin rose his father went on:

'One thing more. Po Het stands on his dignity a bit; but if you are firm with him everything will be all right. Tell him he is to come to see me this evening to discuss moving the logs. The rain will come today, and if we get some normal storms we'll be ready for flooding the river bed within forty-eight hours.'

Martin went out into the brilliant sunshine. He had never expected to be pushed into a position of authority so soon; yet the job had to be done. Their livelihood depended on it, for every penny his father possessed was tied up in this valley.

As he walked across the sunbaked ground towards the village he started to turn over in his mind suitable phrases in Burmese. For years he had been learning the language. His father had a tape recorder, and as regularly as possible he sent tapes home, tapes which carried conversations in Burmese, and their equivalent in English.

At home Martin also had a tape recorder and he sent back monologues in Burmese. It had been slow work for the first year, and then he had suddenly begun to get the feel of the language. During the past year his father had engaged *oozies* in conversation, with the unseen tape recorder picking up every word that was said, and so Martin was able to get not only the words of the language, but the true inflections and pronunciations.

Now that he was going to speak to Po Het, with no father to get him out of any language difficulty, he felt nervous. Yet when he got to the village and asked a small boy to call the headman, the boy never even gave him a

second glance. He turned and ran, obviously understand-
ing every word, and it gave Martin's morale a real boost.

Po Het came hurrying to see what was wanted, and
asked immediately how Martin's father was. On being
assured that the broken legs were the only injury he gave
thanks to Buddha, and hoped the older *thakin* would soon
be on his feet again.

Then Martin told him what he wanted. The *oozies* and
their elephants were to be mustered, and after all breast-
bands had been examined, Po Het was to take them up to
the temple and drag the building to the place allotted.

There was a long silence when Martin finished speaking, and he had a sudden feeling that he had perhaps not
been speaking as well as he ought.

'Have you not understood all I said?' he asked ner-
vously. 'Perhaps I . . . '

'Everything has been well explained, *thakin* Blake,' Po
Het said quietly, 'but to obey your father's commands is
not possible. It is clear to me and the people of this village
that it will be unlucky for us to try to move the temple
again. Think, *thakin* Blake, what has already happened.
Twice jungle *nats* took the buddha from the new temple,
removing it back to its old house. Then, when your father
ordered us to carry the buddha back once more there was
a fire.'

'I know that,' Martin agreed, and felt that his face was
going red.

'The temple he built in this village was burned to ashes,
and the *nats* have once more taken the buddha back to his
old house. Then there was the accident this morning. Why

should breast bands break when even I, who have worked with elephants all my life, have never known it happen. For one breast band to break is unusual, but this morning not only did two breast bands break, but an elephant was injured, and your father is hurt.' He shook his head slowly, and his voice was sombre as he went on : '*Thakin,* we cannot do what you ask, lest much worse fall on us for disobeying.'

'Disobeying!' Martin said angrily. 'If you refuse to do this you will be disobeying my father, who pays your wages. So, take the elephants up the valley and move the temple.'

'*Thakin,* your father has been in Burma a few years,' Po Het had squared his shoulders and there was a fierce frown on his face. 'The buddha has been here for thousands of years. Men come and go – but Buddha is always here. Who must we obey, the white man or Buddha?'

'You must obey my father's orders,' Martin said, trying to speak firmly.

Po Het shook his head.

'I am sorry, *thakin* Blake. No man shall move at my orders to change the position of the buddha's house.'

'But you must realise that if the temple is not moved it will be covered with water when the valley is flooded,' Martin pointed out.

'Then the valley must not be flooded, *thakin,*' Po Het said quietly, and with a little bow – turned away.

Martin acted impulsively. He grabbed the headman by the short sleeve of his gaily coloured shirt and spun him round. Anger flashed in Po Het's eyes, and Martin for a second recoiled. Yet he had to say what was in his mind, and burst out with it.

'There is one thing you may not know, and it is this : if we do not get the teak logs down to the main river my father will be ruined. We are going to get these logs out, and if the temple and its buddha are lost under the flood it will be your fault. You understand . . . your fault.'

A score of men and youths had gathered at a respectful distance to listen, but no one spoke. They were all staring at Martin, as intently as the headman was staring at him.

'Buddha can guard his temple,' Po Het said slowly. 'Has he not already called on the jungle *nats* to move him back to where he loves to be. If water threatens his home . . . maybe the *nats* will even break down Thunder Dam !'

'Thunder Dam?' It was only the second time Martin had heard it called that.

'That is how we name it,' Po Het said quietly, 'for there was much thunder when your father blasted out the foundations. Yet, if Buddha so desires, the dam will be broken with less noise than it was built.'

'You are not going to obey my father's orders?'

'Buddha rules this village, and he has shown that he wishes to stay where he is, neither higher nor lower,' Po Het gave Martin a little salutation, then turned and walked back to his hut. Martin looked at the semi-circle of boys and men, but they turned and hurried away, leaving the young Britisher alone in the narrow village street.

He went back to the bungalow and told his father everything.

'Tcha ! I said Po Het could be awkward,' George Blake

said. 'Humph! And he says Buddha will destroy the dam if we try to flood the valley. Hm!'

'What do you mean by "hm!"?' Martin asked, when the silence stretched on for a full minute.

'There are times when that is all a man *can* say,' his father said quietly. 'Martin, unless a miracle happens we are finished. I've been listening to the mutter of thunder away back in the Shan Hills. The rain will be here tomorrow – and I'll be stretched on this bed – helpless. If they think their temple and buddha are going to be damaged they'll burst the dam wide open. If that happens, we won't even have our fare home!'

He turned on his side, and Martin went out on to the veranda. It was not easy to say anything when a man was facing so complete a ruin of everything he had worked for. His father was an optimist, and if he could see no hope, then the situation was indeed desperate.

There were many hundreds of fine teak logs in the valley, waiting for flood water to send them surging down to the river some miles away. There were storm clouds gathering in the hills, and a dam – Thunder Dam – stretched across the valley to hold back the water from a hundred streams and rills. But if the rising flood reached the temple – Po Het's prophecy was that the jungle *nats* would destroy Thunder Dam.

'There must be something we can do,' Martin muttered angrily, but though he wracked his brain for a solution, he was as empty of ideas when the sun set as when he began torturing himself.

As he sat having his evening meal beside his father's

campbed the first bellow of thunder in their own hills shook the air, and seemed to make the very bamboo of the building tremble. A vivid flash of lightning had lit up the sky a few moments earlier.

'This is it,' his father said, and as he spoke the first of the monsoon storms broke with savage fury.

3

A wild-cat idea

Martin did not expect to sleep at all. For one thing the rain had brought a humidity to the air which made his bedroom seem more like a turkish bath than ever. With only one sheet covering him he lay and soaked in perspiration. The tuktoo lizard was calling away and the rain beat a devil's tattoo on the nipa-palm thatching of the bungalow.

Every few moments flashes of lightning such as Martin had never known before lit the world outside, and sent vivid shafts of light through the venetian-type bamboo blinds. The thunder which followed was like a barrage of heavy artillery. To make it worse, the hills sent the explosions of sound back and forth, so that before one lot of echoes had finished a fresh roar started them off again.

Yet he did sleep. Nature would not be denied, and he had slept little the night before. Tree rats in the thatching scuttled about, fought and played, and sent minute fragments of thatch floating down. The mosquitoes whined incessantly, and Martin slept through it all.

When he awoke he felt almost cold. There was a grey light filtering through the window blind, and the nightlong storm had cooled the air. Martin got up and went to the door. There was an almost frightening silence shrouding everything just now. The rain had ceased about ten minutes before he woke, stopping with a suddenness which suggested that some mighty hand up above had turned off a tap.

The ground looked darker, for some six inches of rain had fallen in the night, and though much of it had drained away towards the shallow river bed which lay between the bungalow and the village, some had managed to soak into the hard earth.

Dawn was coming in, with stray shafts of golden light finding a way through slight breaks in the sullen clouds which seemed to be at war with each other as they tumbled and rolled about. They were the dreaded cumulo-nimbus, whose anvil shaped heads told of the mighty winds raging inside the clouds themselves. Prudent pilots kept their planes on the ground when cumulo-nimbus rode the Burma skies.

A few minutes later the cook appeared with a mug of tea, and apologised for not being earlier. A leak in his cooking shelter had flooded his fireplace and made lighting even the inflammable bamboo kindlings difficult.

'I don't know what you can do today,' Martin's father said, when they were having breakfast. 'You could go up and look at the temple. The trouble is that it is only about ten feet above the valley floor, and ten feet of water in the dam isn't enough to float our logs down.' He finished his last cup of tea and lay down without bothering to light a cheroot. That showed the measure of his worry.

Martin collected an oilskin and sou'wester from the store shed at the back of the bungalow, for though the sun was shining now, and the heavy, lead coloured clouds had retreated to the hills again, his father warned him that it would not last. Once the monsoon broke they could expect rain and rain, and rain.

Martin had a word with the cook before he started out, trying to discover whether there was any chance of getting outside help to enable him to move the temple to a higher spot on the hillside. The cook was sympathetic but shook his head. There were no villages within twenty miles, and in any case no one would dare to interfere. The temple and its buddha belonged to this village.

Telling the man to keep an ear cocked in case there was a call for something from his father, Martin turned and walked up the valley. The dam, half a mile away, did not look very impressive until he got nearer. Then he could see what a titanic job it must have been to build.

His father had blasted holes in the valley floor, and stood tall teak logs in them, wedging them with stones and binding the whole lot together with concrete. Then he had built a sloping bank on each side, facing the centre supports, and in the triangle thus formed had poured hundreds of tons of clay and rubble. It had taken two years to build. At the right season he had cut his trees and hauled them to the banks of the dry river bed. When his dam collected the monsoon rains he could send it all in a surging flood down the rapidly widening valley to the river, sweeping the teak along to the timber wharves some hundreds of miles distant.

He stood on the dam top and looked up the valley. Already there was a difference. Water must have been flooding in throughout the night, for the lake now reached back to where the hills closed in the valley. Already they had a pear-shaped stretch of water which must have been twenty feet deep in the centre of the valley.

Crossing the dam top he strode up the track, scene of yesterday's accident. It was bordered on one side by tall trees, growing right up the hillside, on the other side the ground sloped down to the lake itself. He could see at once that the level of the lake had risen quite a lot, and when he reached the temple could gauge it much better. There had been a gap of eight feet between temple and water the day before. Now the gap was about five feet. A rise of three feet in a night made him raise his eyebrows. It meant there had been an amazing amount of water flowing in off the hills since the rain began – and of course there would be much more to come, even if there was no more rain.

Standing with his back to the temple entrance he looked across the sunlit water and could see the ripples made by a current running down the centre of the lake. The current hit the breast of the dam and divided, one half going to the right, the other to the left and both formed miniature whirlpools.

Carefully lowering himself down the bank he set a white stone at the water's edge, to give him a guide as to the swiftness with which the water level was rising. Scarcely had he got back on to the track than there was a sudden cooling of the air. The sun was blotted out, lightning flashed and thunder bellowed. In seconds rain was sheeting down, and even though he was only a few yards from the temple, by the time he got within its shelter, his head and shoulders were soaking.

The sun had gone as if it had been no more than a picture on a slate over which an unseen hand had wiped a wet cloth. The surface of the lake was pock-marked with a million splashes, and the rain was coming down with such force that it was throwing up mud splashes in front of the temple almost a foot high.

Martin drew back from where a fine mist of water was drifting into the temple and laid a hand on the shoulder of the buddha, even before he quite realised what he was doing. He grinned a little sheepishly after drawing his hand away.

'He doesn't look a bad old stick, anyway,' he murmured, examining the face. It was not the face of a stern and forbidding god. The features were pudgy and smiling. 'You look as if you could be somebody's favourite uncle. The sort who turns up at birthdays with a whacking good present – a pair of football boots, or a cricket bat. I wonder who first shaped you.'

He examined the idol. It was about four feet tall, a pleasantly fat figure squatting on a teak platform. The hands lay idly in the lap, as if the image was getting ready for a short nap.

As he examined the image more closely he noted one or two places where someone had filed off rough places left by the metal workers who cast the buddha. As he rubbed a finger over the rough spots it struck him as being very odd that people could imagine spirits – the *nats* they were so afraid of – could move such a weighty object.

'Whoever moved it did some sweating, I'll bet.' He tapped the buddha with a knuckle, and got a faint 'ping'.

'Hm! It isn't so thick as all that; but I'll bet it weighs a couple of hundredweight, if not more. There were more than one pair of hands busy when you were moved, Mr Buddha. Bet you were carried on a platform or something.'

The idea gave him food for thought. Men had carried the buddha, and as his father had suggested, whoever was behind the movements of the buddha were bent on keeping the teak logs in the valley or, in other words, ruining George Blake.

Martin stood staring at the image for a little while, thinking it over, and growing angrier every moment at the thought that all his father had worked for would be wiped away in one blow if they missed the rains this year.

'You are not going to be drowned, and Thunder Dam isn't going to be smashed, either,' he said. 'I'll save you if I have to tie a flipping lifebelt round your fat tummy. That'd make you look . . . ' and there he stopped. The word 'lifebelt' had given him the germ of an idea.

With Po Het refusing to let the villagers move the temple, there was one other way of keeping the temple and the buddha out of harm's way – suppose he made it into a boat; a kind of Noah's Ark, floating on the flood. If he could do that, then instead of being covered as the level of the lake rose, the whole thing would float.

'And there's enough timber round here to float a battleship,' he said, suddenly feeling better than he had done for the last twenty-four hours. He pulled on his oilskin coat and tied his sou-wester in place, then stepped out into the storm. The rain was so heavy that he instinctively hunched his shoulders as he felt the drops beating on his sou-wester.

He examined the temple. It was about sixteen or seventeen feet square, and built of wood which he thought looked like teak. It had a solid floor, and there was nothing in the building except the buddha. A big carley float underneath would be just the thing, he thought, then shrugged at the craziness of the idea. Where could they get a carley float out here, anyway. He had to think of something else.

He needed a big raft. With rain already beginning to trickle down his neck he thought back to the days when he had built rafts. It had been at a scout training camp. Each competing patrol had been given half a dozen ten-gallon oil drums, a few spars of timber, and told they had to get across a small lake without getting wet or losing any of their equipment.

It had been great fun and quite easy. The six ten-gallon drums had provided an amazing amount of buoyancy, and with the spars lashed across the tops of the drums they had crossed the lake dry foot.

That was it! Oil drums! If he could get enough empty oil drums under the temple, each lashed securely in place, there would be no risk of the rising waters of the lake flooding the buddha.

The idea was like a gift from the gods. It would be the miracle his father had spoken of, for there were plenty of oil drums – fifty-gallon oil drums. They had been flown in with petrol for the cement mixer his father had used when building the big sluice gate in the centre of his dam.

Ignoring the rain he ran quickly back to the bungalow. He fell twice, for the ground was becoming more and more treacherous as the hard baked surface softened to mud, yet kept the rain from soaking deep down. The mud skidded off the untouched ground, and when Martin finally got back to the bungalow he was muddied to the elbows and his legs were brown to the knees.

'I've got a whale of an idea, father,' he said, bursting into his father's room, and poured out his scheme for saving the temple – and so saving their teak. George Blake listened in silence. His legs were throbbing badly, and he had spent a miserable morning. The future had never looked blacker than it did when his son came tearing in.

'You've got to get the drums up to the temple, don't forget,' he pointed out. 'And if Po Het won't co-operate, you've had it. I'm beginning to wonder if he could be the man behind this whole business.'

'Well, don't you think it's worth trying?' Martin asked, disappointment in his voice.

'Of course I do,' his father said. 'Only, I don't want you to be too disappointed if you can't get the job done. Y'know, Martin, I've had lots of time to think while you have been out. We're up against somebody pretty big. I don't think that the villagers would have worried two hoots about the temple if the buddha hadn't been shunted about. I've been in Burma too long not to know a little bit about the people. There's someone behind this who is prepared to go a long way to stop us getting our teak out.'

'Well, I can try, can't I? If it doesn't come off . . . well,' and Martin shrugged.

'Get your wet things off, and have some lunch, then go down immediately afterwards,' his father suggested. 'When you go out next time, take a thick towel to wrap round your neck. It stops the rain from dripping down your back and chest. I don't want to have to start doctoring you. You can get pneumonia easy enough at this time of the year . . . hot at night, then cool in the morning, and your bed sheets damp with perspiration. We don't want your mother worrying over *two* invalids, do we?'

Martin was rather silent during the mid-day meal. It had startled him to think how easily he had forgotten his mother and his sister. There had been so much to think about and do since he got here that he had never given them a thought.

The rain had ceased when he strode down to the village. Children were playing, and it reminded him of home when he saw two tiny tots making mud-pies. For most of the year there was not enough water to make mud, and they were enjoying this pastime as much as children who make sand pies at a British holiday resort.

Going straight to the headman's hut Martin called for Po Het, and when he came out told him he wanted labour immediately. The men were to bring some of the elephants across to the bungalow to pick up oil drums and digging tools – picks and spades.

Po Het shouted to a boy standing near, and within five minutes the call was going from hut to hut that the men were needed. Martin waited until all was quiet, then explained what he proposed to do. The men were to dig a space beneath the temple so that oil drums could be put underneath to form a raft on which the building would float when the lake level rose high enough.

All eyes turned to Po Het when Martin finished, and it was obvious at once that the *oozies* were uneasy. The headman held the key to the situation. If he said 'Yes' the work would be done; and they were waiting for him to give a sign. Po Het remained silent, staring down at his feet as if he found them very interesting indeed.

'There will be extra pay for this,' Martin promised, 'and remember – if we get the teak logs down to the river during the next few days it will mean that my father and I will stay here for a long time – and there will be constant work for everyone, for years to come.'

Again there was silence, until Po Het suddenly looked up and said defiantly :

'You are too young to understand, *thakin* Blake. Yesterday an elephant was hurt and an *oozie* almost drowned. Your own father, whom we all love, suffered an injury. It is bad luck to do anything to the temple. If we start trying to dig under it worse things may happen. Do you not understand that the jungle *nats* are angry? It is time for plain speaking. A man who risks his life for timber is a fool.'

Martin flushed. In any other circumstances he would probably have been afraid to show anger to these men, but the thought that his father would be ruined if they did not get the teak out made him forget his youth and his fears. Hands on hips he glared at Po Het and there was disgust in his voice when he snapped :

'You talk like a child. *I* am not afraid of jungle *nats,* and *I* am going to work on the temple. As for you,' and he turned to face the half circle of men and youths. 'Those who love my father, and have worked for him for so long, if you have any loyalty towards him, you will come with me. I have said there will be extra pay and it will mean work for a long time if you help us now.'

He looked around the half ring of faces, but whenever he caught the eyes of a man, that man looked down. Neither loyalty nor the promise of extra pay was going to induce any of them to risk the wrath of Po Het, and the *nats*.

Then a slim youngster pushed his way through to the centre of the open space and, saluting Martin, said quietly:

'*Thakin*, yesterday you saved the life of my father. He has worked for your father for many years. Today he is feeling sick, so must rest. I know he would help you if he were well. I am San Shwe. Tell me what you want me to do, and I will do it.'

Po Het gave an angry shout, ordering the boy back.

'Will you bring the anger of the *nats* on all of us?' he demanded. 'You must give a thought to your own people. We are always here. The *thakin* does not care. One day he will go home – perhaps there are no jungle *nats* where he lives.'

San Shwe, obviously rather nervous, faced the headman saying:

'Po Het, you are headman of this village, and a man to be respected – but are we to eat the white man's rice, and then turn our back on him when he is in trouble? Even a dog does not bite the hand that feeds him.' Turning to

Martin he said: 'I can ride my father's elephant – if you need him.'

'Yes, harness him and bring him here,' and to Po Het he said coldly, 'I am going back to speak to my father about you. And do not think that he is so badly hurt that he does not know what is happening. Men who refuse to work may also find there is no money for them when pay day comes.'

There was an audible hissing of indrawn breaths at that, and Martin realised he had scored a valuable point. To Po Het he said sternly:

'I shall come back in a few minutes. Think well of what I have said,' and turning on his heel he strode away.

However bold and resolute he may have appeared when addressing the Burmese, he was shaking as he approached the bungalow. Anger had spurred him on, but the anger was cooling now, and he wondered if he had gone too far. Did one say things like that to a headman? Martin had an uneasy feeling that people like Po Het were treated with much greater respect, especially when their own people were standing by.

He told his father what had happened, and George Blake pursed his lips. Martin had gone a little too far, but there could be no drawing back. Having said he would do something, he had to go on with it.

'You have asked him fairly,' George said, 'and you have told him the consequences if he doesn't help. The best thing now is to go back – be cool, polite, and if he still re-fuses to co-operate you had better tell him that he is no longer working for us.'

'Had I better take the – the revolver?' Martin asked.

'Good lor', no,' his father said hastily. 'No, these people are ruled by respect. You don't threaten them. In a way I suppose you threatened him about his pay, but that he would understand. No work, no rupees. You must just go down there, ask him if he has changed his mind, and if he still refuses to work, take the boy who has offered to help, and come back here for the oil drums.'

'And say nothing of the pay, or that he is sacked?'

'No, leave him to worry about that,' Martin's father said. 'Sometimes it is better that way. He'll maybe come up here to have a word with me. Now, remember, above all, keep calm. If Po Het wants to get angry, let him. The chap who keeps his temper has a big advantage. Now, off you go and don't worry.'

'Don't worry,' Martin exploded. 'Father, don't you rea-lise that . . . '

'I realise what is going on,' his father said, smiling rue-fully. 'I have been in Burma a little while, you know. The great thing is – don't worry. Go down there and let them see that nothing is upsetting you. That's the great thing when there is trouble brewing.'

Yet when Martin had moved out on to the veranda George Blake ran a hand through his grizzling hair and shook his head. To be laid up when a situation like this had arisen was almost more than he could bear. To have to send his inexperienced son out to try and clear up the trouble was the bitterest thing he had ever had to do. Yet it was that or acknowledge defeat.

With great care he eased his splinted legs into a more

comfortable position, then lay back, eyes closed. He knew
that one way or another the matter would be settled within the next thirty-six hours. Either Martin would win, and
the villagers would help him – and that would mean the
logs would be got out. Or, Po Het would win and that
meant ruin.

On the veranda Martin was staring across the valley towards the village. He was trying to make up his mind to
go across there, yet he was afraid. For the moment the day
was calm and windless. The sun was shining, though
more banks of leaden cloud were beginning to pile up over
the hills. There was a stillness about everything, a kind of
hush, and as that word came into his mind, it conjured up
an almost forgotten poem. Once it had been his favourite,
and the first lines came back easily. It concerned a cricket
match and a crisis:

> *There's a breathless hush in the close tonight*
> *Ten to make and a match to win*
> *A bumping pitch and a blinding light*
> *An hour to play and the last man in.*

As he stood on the top of the veranda steps the words
brought back to him the old dream of being the hero of
the hour. Many a time in bed he had gone through the
thrill of making that dream come true. He had been 'the
last man in'. He had been the one to face the opposing
team's demon bowler.

While schoolmates and supporters of both teams waited
round the edge of the field, waiting for the first ball to
shatter Martin's wicket, and finish the match, the boy

whom no one thought could face such a crisis had played ball after ball. Then, finally choosing the right one, he had opened his shoulders and lofted the ball out of the ground for a magnificent six. A coolly taken four off the next ball, and Martin Blake had been the hero of the hour. The 'rabbit' who had won the match.

His dream had never come true. Somehow he had never been asked to make a do-or-die stand. His triumphs had never been more than dreams. The clatter of an enamel mug falling from the cook's hand into the bucket brought him out of his reverie, and he hurriedly walked down the steps of the veranda, wondering guiltily if his father was thinking his son was afraid to go down and face Po Het.

'And you are afraid, you know,' he told himself, walking very slowly away from the bungalow. His hands went automatically to his pockets and he stopped. Somehow the very fact of saying that he was afraid had made it seem hopeless to go on. Then the cook, without knowing it, came to his aid. He called out:

'Must I stay and look after the master?'

'Yes . . . I am going down to the village.' It was out, and there was no turning back unless he wanted the cook to know that *thakin* Blake's son was a coward. To himself he muttered: 'And I'll bet they are all down there, waiting to see what I will do!' Then, suddenly desperate, he squared his shoulders and strode purposefully across the wet ground.

As he drew nearer the village he saw activity. A boy had been posted to watch for his coming and he was running down the short narrow street shouting:

'The young *thakin* is coming. The young *thakin* is coming.'

As Martin drew nearer he saw men and women coming to the doors of the huts, and realised there was going to be a showdown. There must have been some kind of a meeting, and they had come to a decision – hence the spy to report when the young *thakin* was on his way.

His heart was sinking as he strode between two huts and into the village street.

4

Martin wins -

Everyone was out. Women leaned against their hut doors,
many of them holding a baby. Children who would normally have been playing were gathered by their own hut.
The men were squatting in little groups, smoking cigar-
ettes, and all eyes were on the young Englishman.

Po Het was not to be seen, and Martin turned and strode
vigorously up to the headman's hut. He was taut nerved,
forcing himself to give an impression of determination,
but there was a dew of sweat on his upper lip.

As he drew near the hut the headman came to the door.
He was smoking a pipe. The bowl was of baked clay and
the stem a piece of thin cane. Instead of coming out to
greet Martin, the headman stood there, puffing smoke and
staring.

Then Martin made a mistake. Despite his determination
his steps had faltered, and the headman said something to
his wife, who was standing just inside the hut. Her reaction was immediate: a shrill peal of laughter, stifled within seconds as if she had clapped a hand across her mouth.

Someone else laughed, and the joke, whatever it was,
seemed to pass from group to group. The men chuckled,
then looked down and were silent when Martin turned to
stare at them. Despite what had been said they still respected the authority of the white man, even if he was only a
youth with hardly a hair on his chin.

Martin turned to Po Het. He walked quietly nearer, and when he was no more than five feet from the headman, asked:

'I am giving you another chance. Have you changed your mind?'

It was disrespectful not to give him his title, or address him by name, and in the five or six seconds which followed before the headman gave his reply there was an air of hushed expectancy over the village. The sniggers and chuckles died away. Everyone, down to the youngest child, seemed to be waiting, as if they knew that this was a moment to be remembered.

Po Het's reply was deliberate. He took his pipe from his mouth and spat on the ground. Whether he was getting ready to speak, or whether what he did was a deliberate insult, only he knew. If Martin had remembered his father's advice to keep cool, and calm, he might have turned on his heels. Instead he glared at the headman and said acidly:

'Po Het, you were my father's headman, I think!'

Po Het stiffened, and Martin sensed the movements among the men. Those who had been squatting on their heels began to rise, sensing some dramatic development. A woman at the door of a nearby hut ushered two young children inside, and followed them.

'You said *were, thakin*,' Po Het said angrily. 'I say I *am* the headman of this village. The people do as I tell them. If you have come for that poor fool San Shwe, I will tell you that he is sitting in his father's hut . . . and he stays there. I have told him to stay there. No one is to go up to

the temple . . . and if you are wise you will open the gates in Thunder Dam so that no water can reach either temple or Buddha. I have spoken.'

'And now I shall speak,' Martin snapped. 'I am ordering you to call San Shwe out. He is to help me . . . and bring his father's elephant. And remember this, the elephants do not belong to you. They are my father's property.'

'Then you can ride them yourself,' Po Het jeered.

'You are not going to do as I ask?'

'I have said all I am going to say. Now I go to my hut to rest.'

'Then you can rest for a long time,' Martin shouted. 'My father no longer needs you as headman. You are discharged, and will no longer draw wages. From this . . . ' and that was as far as he got.

Sudden fury in his eyes, Po Het turned and snatched up his *dah* which had been standing, unsheathed, against the side post of the hut door. Wild with rage he swung round, the twenty-inch blade gleaming in the sunlight.

There were gasps of horror from men and one woman screamed. Martin scarcely heard anything. He did the only thing possible. Instead of trying to run he lunged forward, ducking to avoid the swinging blade.

He was wearing a floppy hat, such as is issued to British troops on jungle duty, but that scarcely cushioned the effect of his head striking Po Het in the stomach. The blow was doubly severe because the headman was moving forward.

The whole incident lasted no more than ten seconds,

and when Martin reeled back the headman was rolling over on the ground, his knees drawn up, his mouth wide open as he gasped for air. The unintentional butt had been like a perfectly delivered solar plexus punch, driving all the air out of the headman's lungs and temporarily paralysing him. His *dah* had dropped to the ground, and for a moment Martin was tempted to make a grab for it.

He resisted the temptation and spinning round faced the nearest group of men. He was quaking inwardly, and a hostile move might have sent him in retreat; but there was no hostile move. Silent, goggle-eyed, men, women and children stared at their headman, and within seconds Martin's whole outlook changed. He had won. He knew it without anyone saying a word.

'Where is the boy San Shwe?' Martin asked, walking towards the nearest group of men. 'Call him.'

The men backed away, but one of them turned and yelled for San Shwe. A few moments later the young Burmese peered out from a hut about twenty yards away. He had seen nothing of what had happened, and gaped when he saw the prostrate figure of Po Het.

Martin strode towards the boy. In a firm voice he ordered him to bring his elephant. San Shwe looked at Martin, looked past him at the headman, still squirming on the ground, and then he gave the usual little salutation and turning, ran through a gap between two huts.

The next ten minutes were among the longest Martin ever knew. Po Het's wife had come out, and was kneeling by her husband. He was still in a jack-knifed position, and was with difficulty getting back his breath. When she managed to get him to his feet he stumbled into the hut.

Martin was tempted to appeal to the men to help him, but decided against it. No one moved, no one spoke. When Martin chanced to catch the eye of one of the *oozies,* the man lowered his gaze. Then, from somewhere near the trees there came a loud 'Yooumph!' It was San Shwe making his elephant trumpet to show that he was obeying Martin's orders.

A minute or so later the huge tusker made his slow, majestic way between two huts and into the village street. At a word of command he sank to his knees and San Shwe looked at Martin, saying nothing but obviously expecting the young Britisher to join him on the elephant's back. In a strained silence Martin climbed up. It was only the second time in his life he had ridden such a huge beast, the first time being years earlier at a zoo. Then he had sat in a special seat made to hold three children on each side of the elephant. This time he sat behind San Shwe, straddled across the thick neck.

A word to the tusker and they were on the move. They crossed the river bed and stopped only when they reached the bungalow. Martin dismounted and went in to report to his father, and George Blake's face was bleak as he listened to the account of how Po Het had swung a *dah* at his son. It increased the gravity of the situation but he tried to hide his concern. With a nod he agreed that sacking the headman had been unavoidable, and when he had heard the full story he said:

'I don't want to frighten you, Martin, but I think it might be a good idea if you took your revolver with you from now on. Keep the safety catch on. Sight of a gun is often enough to overawe a trouble maker. If you do have to shoot – and I hope to goodness it doesn't come to that – aim low. Don't forget that – aim low. But only bring your gun out if the situation becomes really desperate. I imagine Po Het could have been taught a lesson.'

For Martin it was an odd feeling to fasten a revolver to his waist. It was almost as if he was getting ready to take part in a threatrical drama, and not the real thing. When he went out he half expected San Shwe to comment, but the young Burmese was too busy rolling fifty-gallon oil drums out of the store shed. If he saw the revolver he gave no sign.

It took them half an hour to get two dozen empty drums lashed to the back of the elephant. They added two picks and two spades to the load, then started off for the temple.

By this time thunder was booming in the hills and the sky, which had been fairly clear of cloud was filling up again. The sun was suddenly obscured and within seconds there was a coolness in the air. Then the rain began once more.

Wearing only a thin bush jacket over his string vest and shorts, Martin was soon dripping wet, yet he knew an odd exhilaration as he walked beside the big bull elephant. The rain drops beat a tattoo on the empty oil drums, and the big feet of the tusker threw up masses of brown mud.

Lightning slashed the leaden clouds which lay low over the tree covered hilltops, and when they were crossing the end of the dam a particularly vicious blue-white tongue licked down in front of them and seemed to explode like a high calibre shell with a report which shocked the ear drums.

Even the elephant hesitated, and a few seconds later there was a disturbance in the trees ahead. Then a giant sal tree crashed through its neighbours to the ground, riven from top down to the roots by the terrible force of the electrical discharge. The timber was smoking as Martin and San Shwe paused for a moment to look at it. The young Burmese had seen this kind of thing before; but it was new to Martin. He had read accounts of cattle being struck by lightning when sheltering under trees; of houses being damaged in similar fashion; but he had never realised just what awful power there was in a shaft of lightning.

It was a positive relief when they reached the temple and could begin work. It helped to take his thoughts off the lightning, and the dangers attending anyone working near these tall, rain soaked trees. San Shwe tethered the elephant to a young teak tree, and with the twenty-four empty oil drums stacked near, Martin and his assistant tackled the job of digging out beneath the temple.

The spades were useless except for moving away the earth they broke up with the picks. Though the ground all around was soaked, that sheltered by the temple itself was still iron hard.

In half an hour, during which time the skin of his hands began to ridge and redden, Martin dug out less than a yard of earth. San Shwe did little better, for he was more accustomed to handling elephant chains than a pick.

The rain stopped once more, leaving a steamy heat which Martin found more exhausting. Perspiration poured out of him, and he developed a raging thirst. Yet when he looked longingly at the lake water he decided not to drink. It was muddy from the torrents rolling into it further up the valley.

He had just stopped to straighten his aching back and pat his blistering palms against his wet shirt, when San Shwe gave a little yelp and pointed along the track. Martin turned, and his heart gave a sudden bound for coming towards them were Po Het and the *oozies*. At least two dozen men, with a group of chain boys following some distance behind.

For a moment Martin panicked, remembering what he had done to the headman. He had humiliated him before his own people, a thing not easily forgotten or forgiven. Then he remembered his revolver. His hand slipped down to the webbing holster. He whipped the flap open, then in an effort to appear calm and unafraid he put his hands on his hips and waited.

Po Het's eyes had not missed the significance of Martin's hand movements. Nor had he failed to see the revolver. He slowed down, then stopped. The men behind bunched close, and for perhaps a minute there was silence. A silence broken when Martin called:

'You wish to see me, Po Het?'

The headman half turned, obviously to say something to the men behind him, then he started to come on, the *oozies* following close on his heels. Martin hitched up his belt, an action which must have seemed to the Burmese like the preliminary to drawing the revolver, for they stopped.

Then, at a word from Po Het, they came on again, more slowly, but like a procession which is not to be stopped. San Shwe moved round so that Martin was between him and the *oozies,* and there was terror in his voice when he whispered:

'*Thakin* . . . the gun. Get your gun out before it is too late.'

- and Po Het strikes

When they were a dozen feet from Martin the procession halted. Then, to the astonishment of the young Britisher, Po Het clapped his hands together in the usual salutation, and said humbly:

'*Thakin* Blake, I have come to ask for pardon. I have been wrong. I wish to work for you, and be headman once more for your father.'

It was so exactly opposite to what Martin was expecting that it took him several seconds to collect his wits. He had expected arrogance, threats, perhaps even an ultimatum. Oddly enough, his silence had its effect on Po Het, for he went on coaxingly:

'*Thakin,* no man is perfect. I was worried, and afraid. Now I see that I was wrong. Forgive me, for if I cannot work for you and your father then I am a man without authority, and will starve.'

In that moment he appeared to Martin exactly as he had appeared when they first met on the long untilled paddy field where the little Auster aircraft had made its bumpy landing. His wrinkled face carried a light stubble of greying beard, and wore an anxious expression, half pleading, half coaxing. As if he wanted to give a good impression.

'You know the work that I am doing,' Martin said, trying not to let his relief and triumph show. 'There are tools here for only four men. Send two men back to the store hut, and the cook will give them enough spades and picks for everyone. The ground beneath the temple must be dug away to a depth which will allow us to put these oil drums beneath. You understand?'

'Yes, *thakin*. The drums are to be tied under the floor of the temple, so that when the waters rise the temple will float. You have not brought ropes. Shall the men bring ropes as well as picks and spades?'

'Yes!' Martin was a little annoyed that the headman should have so quickly spotted one of the deficiencies in his scheme. Nevertheless it was a relief to be able to hand over the pick he had been using, and soothe his aching hands with a pack of mud. He could not have kept on digging for much longer, for the tender skin was already showing signs of blistering.

Until the sun set, despite intermittent downpours of rain, the men worked unceasing. Po Het proved himself a master 'foreman'. He seemed to know to the moment when the men working under the temple needed a rest. He would call them out and send a new gang under.

As they dug out, they rolled drum after drum under the temple, jamming them between earth and floor timbers. Before each drum went in Martin examined it to make sure it was intact, and he insisted on unscrewing the cap, then screwing it back again as tightly as possible. Each one must be absolutely watertight.

The drums were secured by ropes attached to the planking under the floor of the temple-planking which had been put there initially to act as a sledge when Martin's father had hoped to drag the temple to a safer position.

It was San Shwe's father, the man Martin had rescued, who came forward with an idea for ensuring maximum security for the temple. He suggested that ropes should be fastened round the wooden building, and passed round stout trees growing on the hillside. This would ensure that when the temple did float, it would not drift away into the middle of the lake.

In a hissing downpour, when it was growing too dark to see what was being done, Martin called a halt. Had he and San Shwe been left to dig out alone they would have found the task far too big for them. As it was, another hour or so would see the whole operation completed.

To Po Het he said:

'The men can go back to their homes now for food but they must return in two hours' time. The job must be finished this evening. The lake level is rising so quickly that it is possible the temple could be afloat by dawn. Tell them there will be extra pay from my father at the end of the month. They have worked very well, and it will not be forgotten.'

'The work will be finished before the men lie down to sleep, *thakin*,' Po Het promised, and looking up at the darkening skies for a moment he added: 'There is much more rain to come, and the lake will have risen very high by morning.' He gave Martin the usual parting salutation, called to the weary men, and then led the way back towards the village.

'You had better go back with them,' Martin told San Shwe, and added a little guiltily. 'Keep your ears open. I

am not sure whether I can trust Po Het. If you hear anything you think would interest me . . . come to the bungalow at once.'

'Yes, *thakin*,' and with that the willowy Burmese youth
turned and trotted up the slippery track after the others.

Martin was weary and leaden-footed when he got back
to the bungalow. Excitement had kept him going, but
now he was feeling the effects of the long day. For the
moment the rain had ceased, and there were a few clear
patches in the sky through which stars were beginning to
show.

His wet clothes clung to him and he shivered as he went
up the three steps to the veranda. Going into his father's
room he held up a thumb as a sign that all was going well.

'Don't tell me now,' his father said gruffly, to hide an
emotion which had been building up from the moment
the men had come for the tools and the ropes. 'I have told
the cook to prepare a hot bath for you. Have a good soak,
and don't come in to see me until you are in clean dry
clothes.'

It was good advice. The cook had two empty oil drums
standing over a roaring fire of split bamboo, and within
minutes of leaving his father's room Martin was lowering
himself gingerly into the canvas camp bath. The cook was
waiting with a can of cold water in case the bath proved
too hot.

Martin poured hot water over his head and shoulders,
and by the time he was ready for the big towel the cook
was warming, he felt immeasurably better. The soaking
had rid him of many of his aches and pains. Now he was

hungry but he also had a feeling of tremendous optimism. If the morning had started badly, the day was ending well.

He rubbed himself down, and then because the dampness of the atmosphere made body drying so difficult, he reached for the big tin of talcum powder which the cook had left, saying that '*Thakin* Blake says you will find this useful after the bath.'

Looking at the tin Martin grinned at the idea of using talcum.

'If the fellows at home could see me using this they'd never let it drop,' he chuckled. 'Sissy stuff. Still, I suppose if my father uses it I can try it,' and he shook a liberal cloud of powder on his damp skin. It did what even the dry towel had failed to do, and when he slipped into clean clothes he felt like a new man.

In his father's room the table had been laid for the evening meal, and under the paraffin pressure lamp it was almost possible to forget that they were many miles from civilization. The cloth was white, the cutlery winked silvery in the light, and there were even napkins.

'You have to keep up this standard,' his father said, guessing what was going through Martin's mind. 'If you didn't it would be so easy to slip into being a jungle slut. And this kind of thing has its effect on the men who work for you. When you keep yourself spruce, when you demand cleanliness in everything, they give you the respect they think is due to a great "*thakin*"!' and he winked.

George Blake's legs were still giving him pain, but he was hoping that in the next day or so a doctor might arrive. It would mean making short plane hops between the showers, but Hodgson, the doctor at Akyab, was always prepared to do that kind of thing when a serious accident had occurred – especially if it was up country where treatment was difficult, and the patient could not travel.

Over coffee Martin's father smoked a cheroot, sure sign that he was feeling much better mentally. Then came the moment when Martin had to go out once more, to see the temple job finished. The cook was busy in his shelter. He had washed Martin's dirty shirt, shorts, vest and socks, and was drying them by ironing with an old type flat-iron heated in the embers of his fire. There would be a fresh change of dry clothing when Martin returned.

Lighting his way by means of his big torch Martin was delighted to see across the valley a string of tiny lights heading eastwards. The villagers were on time. Po Het was keeping his promise.

They worked until just after ten o'clock, and when the last big oil drum had been tied in place the lake had risen until it was starting to lap over into the area they had dug out.

'By morning the temple will be floating, *thakin*,' Po Het promised as he went with Martin to check the anchorage ropes which would prevent the temple from floating away. 'Everything very good?'

'Fine,' Martin agreed, 'and thank you for your help, *U* Po Het.' The 'U' was a politeness offered to people of importance. The headman gave a little start, smiled, then bowed his acknowledgment, and Martin felt even better than before. He was sure he had scored a hit with the headman by that simple little courtesy. His father had told him often enough about this courtesy which was offered at times to show the man addressed that he was of some importance.

They left the temple site and made their way back, crossing the end of the dam and dropping down the other side to the lower part of the valley. Martin trudged back to the bungalow, had another bath, reported progress to his father, and went to bed.

Thunder was beginning its muttering promise of more rain when he tucked in his mosquito netting. The tuktoo lizard which he had not yet seen, began calling the moment he turned his lamp out, but within minutes he was asleep. The room was hot and humid. The bed felt damp. It was an uncomfortable turkish bath atmosphere, but sheer physical tiredness, plus the fact that he had had a day ending in triumph, helped him ignore everything.

The thunder bellowed overhead; vivid flashes of lightning sent shafts of white streaming through the split-bamboo blinds, and rain beat a continuous tattoo on the nipa-palm thatching, but Martin heard none of it.

*

Across in the village Po Het went to his hut and stayed there for an hour. When he finally looked out the rain was hissing down, and there was not a single light showing in any of the huts. It had been an afternoon and evening of harder than usual work, and the *oozies* and the younger *pajaiks* were all asleep.

Po Het's wife was asleep, and never heard her husband fill the little oil lamp then take his *dah* from the nail driven into one of the wall supports. With nothing to cover him he walked out into the pouring rain.

Not until he was well clear of the village did he pause and after several attempts, light his lamp. He held a big leaf on one side of it so that if anyone in the white man's bungalow should chance to look out he would not see a strange pinpoint of light going up the valley.

When he was within a hundred yards of the temple he was almost turned back, for out of the jungle covered hillside, his coat shining in the rain when lightning flashed, came a mighty sambar stag. He almost ran into the lake, turning at the last second as lightning showed him the valley now covered with water.

Behind him, only seconds later, came a tiger. Po Het saw both animals by the almost continuous flashes of lightning, and sank to his knees, shielding his lamp; his eyes were round with fear and his mouth was agape. Fortunately for him the tiger had eyes only for the big stag. He had already drawn blood with a badly timed spring, and was anxious now to make a kill.

Hunted and hunter bounded up the trail. They turned aside when they came to the temple and were lost to sight and sound in less than a minute; but it took Po Het several minutes to get back his nerve.

Like most men who live on the fringe of the Burmese jungles he firmly believed in the existence of *nats,* but it was fear of something even worse which had nerved him to come out, alone, this night. When he had at last stilled the shaking of his hands he went cautiously on to the temple.

Standing his lamp on the temple floor he stood for a few moments staring at the brass buddha. Then, as if hypnotised by the gently smiling face, he shuffled on his knees until by bending he could lay his forehead at the feet of the image.

'It is not of my own will, O Great One, that you are to go into the waters,' he whispered. 'There is someone who could harm me who forces me to this. He has paid me money – and now commands me to do this thing, or I shall be taken away and cast into a prison. Have mercy on me,' and he banged his forehead a dozen times on the unresponding brass.

Then he got to his feet, went outside again to splash ankle deep in water now beginning to flood under the floor of the temple. The black oil drums were all standing in three or four inches of water. The lake was rising very quickly, and would keep on rising. Rain was slashing down in the hills, turning every rill into a freshet, every stream into a roaring flood.

Finding a stone on which to stand his lamp, Po Het crawled under the temple. Unsheathing his *dah* he steadied himself in his crouched position for a blow, and a few seconds later there was a deep, gong-like note as the heavy blade struck the nearest oil drum just above the level of the water.

Moving his lamp nearer he examined the result and nodded his satisfaction. The *dah*, though made of relatively soft iron, had not only dented the drum, but split the sheet metal. He struck the drum as close to the top as possible, making another split. That would enable water to flow in at the bottom and air to seep out at the top.

In half an hour he had treated ten of the drums, and by that time his whole body was aching with fatigue. It was back- and arm-breaking work to strike the powerful blows needed to puncture the drums, while crouching in a half doubled-up position.

'It will surely sink, now,' he decided, and splashed his way out into the open again. In the thirty minutes he had been working there the water level had risen four to five inches. It was so high that he could see it draining into the first drums he had punctured.

About to move off he remembered the buddha, and went once more into the temple. With his lamp standing nearby he prostrated himself again, knocking his head on the buddha's feet, and pleading for forgiveness.

'When it is all over, and the water has gone, then I promise this house shall be raised again to this place, and you shall be brought back to live here in peace for all time.'

His face was very solemn as he turned and left the temple. To drown a buddha, even if only for a few days, was no light thing, and Po Het's face was haggard as he walked wearily back to the village.

He lay down but could not sleep, and when the first wet jungle cock broke the silence of a dawn which was now without rain, Po Het rose and to his wife's astonishment lit the cooking fire. He would have gone up the valley as soon as he had eaten rice if he had dared, but that might have brought comment. Instead, he filled his pipe and waited.

6

A buddha in danger

Martin was asleep when the cook brought the first cup of tea, and when the mosquito netting was drawn aside he found it hard to realise that he was in the same world. Brilliant sunshine was streaming through the open door, and as on his first morning here, there was a cheerful chatter of birds as a flock of the yellow and black minahs, the eastern counterpart of the British starling, were wrangling over scraps from the kitchen.

'It is fine!' Martin said, amazed, and the cook smiled and nodded.

'Better day this day, *thakin,* than yesterday,' he agreed. 'It rained very hard in night. You did not hear?'

'Never heard a thing,' Martin said, sipping the steaming tea. He sat on the edge of the campbed for a minute or so, then stripped and sluiced down on the veranda. It was a marvellous day. For the time being, at least, it looked as if the monsoon clouds had taken a holiday. The sky had only one or two wisps of white cloud and for the rest it was a dazzling blue.

'Martin, come in when you are dressed. It has been a shocking night, and I think you should go and look at the temple as soon as possible.'

'I'll go up right away,' Martin promised, hurrying into his father's room with his towel wrapped about him. 'I can be there and back in less than an hour.'

'No, have some breakfast first,' his father said, and Martin frowned as he saw the lines of fatigue on the older man's face. 'I haven't had a good night. The legs were a bit achy, so I heard all the rain. Until about an hour ago it never ceased. I'm worried about the temple, and I'm worried about the dam.'

'Why the dam?' Martin queried. 'There's nothing wrong with it, is there?'

'Don't forget it's an amateur's job,' his father reminded him. 'I got all the advice I could, of course, and studied some technical books on the subject too. But I'm worried. If it gets too much water in it . . . the whole thing might go. If that happened lives would be lost. The village isn't so much higher than the river bed. A big flood could catch them.'

'I'll get dressed at once,' and Martin hurried round to his own room. He was as good as his word, dressing in record time while his father was calling to the cook to hurry on the breakfast.

Martin was anxious about his father, and the pain.

'I think I must have got a bit restless,' his father said, shrugging. 'I just couldn't sleep, and when you can't sleep you start worrying. Anyway, get up to the temple, and if that's all right, send the *oozies* with their elephants down-river. Po Het will know where to station them. If the lake is within ten feet of the top of the dam you can open the sluice gate – open it wide, and keep it open for an hour. Then close it and let the level build up again.'

'Will they have got all the logs out by then?' Martin asked astonished.

'No, but they should have got most of them moving. Then, while the level builds up in the valley again they can free any jammed logs, and get ready for the next water you send down.'

Martin gulped down his second cup of tea and was rising when his father said, almost hesitantly, as if it was something he hardly cared to think about:

'If there is any danger to the temple – you know, if your plan for floating it has gone wrong – don't hesitate to open the sluice gate. Lower the level of the lake, even if the *oozies* aren't ready to go to work.' And as Martin hesitated, he went on urgently, 'There's more to it than just drowning a brass image, Martin. Whatever you may think about Buddhism, these people believe in it. It is their religion, and they are devout people. You are not to risk anything happening to the buddha. If it means losing all our water . . . and going bankrupt, nothing must happen to it or the temple.'

Martin nodded. His father's seriousness had taken some of the joy out of the morning, and given him a premonition of disaster ahead.

As he strode diagonally across the muddy fields towards the far side of the dam and the track leading up to the temple he could see several *oozies* moving up in the same direction. That set a little alarm bell ringing at the back of his mind. Why were they going up to the temple? There was no reason for it unless they knew something had gone wrong.

'Perhaps they just want to see if the temple will really float,' he murmured, trying to reassure himself. 'After all, it is their church, and I suppose they are anxious to see if everything is all right.'

The men were ahead of him when he crossed the dam, and it was then that he got his first inkling of how high the level of the water had risen during the night. The track leading to the temple was under water. It meant he had to walk through the fringe of trees and shrubs.

He passed one spot where the ground was red with the petals of the flame-of-the-forest tree, and when he looked up there was not one bloom left. Every flower had been beaten off by the continued deluge.

'They don't last long,' he murmured, stooping as he walked to pick up a petal. 'Folks back home would go crazy to have a tree like this in the garden. It would be a picture.'

A yell from somewhere ahead took his mind off such pleasant thoughts, and he hurried through the trees as the caller yelled again, a note of desperate urgency in his voice:

'*Thakin . . . thakin . . . THAKIN*! Hurry.'

Martin began to run, though on the wet sloping ground it was inviting a fall. Twice he slid, and might have ended up in the water but for being able to grab at the branch of a tree. He carried on with more care after shouting that he was coming.

Then, almost before he realised it, he was near the temple, and his heart sank. A score of rather frightened *oozies* were there, looking anxiously at him as he walked cautiously down the slippery slope. One foot slipped and he made a hasty grab at a rope, one of the two anchor ropes they had fixed up the night before. They were fastened to the temple and then to two stout trees.

Martin's first reaction as he clutched at the rope to steady himself was that it was trembling, yet taut as a bar of iron. It was under a tremendous strain. Then he looked at the temple, and his heart almost stopped beating.

He could not decide for the moment what was wrong, for he could see far more of the back of the building than he ought to. Then he realised that it was tilted forward; the chief reason for the tremendous strain on the two mooring ropes.

'It is going to slip into the lake, *thakin*!' the speaker was Po Het, and his voice was bleak and frightened. 'What can we do? You promised that the temple would not be drowned, and now it is going to slide off this track and into the lake.'

Martin eased himself down until he was standing at the edge of the water. The lake had risen almost four feet since he had last stood by the temple, and the track was under three feet of water. The front of the temple did not seem to have risen at all, but the back was up. Something had gone wrong with his plan to give the whole thing buoyancy.

With all eyes on him Martin lowered himself into the water, steadied by young San Shwe who seemed to be the only one there who was not petrified with horror.

'Be careful, *thakin*,' San Shwe cautioned. 'There may be a *Nat Shin* swimming near.'

'*Shin*?' Martin said, frowning, and then remembered. *Shin* meant snake. Well, he was not afraid of snake spirits, and he waded to the front of the temple. If he had been worried before, he was more so now. Due to the tilt of the temple floor the brass buddha had slid forward and it was poised now on the edge of the doorway.

It looked like a fat old man contemplating a plunge. Yet if it did plunge into the lake it would be the last straw. Remembering how worried his father had been about the safety of the temple and the buddha Martin's mind almost stopped working. His father had spoken of lowering the level of the lake by opening the sluice gate if there was any real danger to the temple, but short of the dam bursting it was quite impossible to lower the level of the water quickly enough to save this situation.

If the temple front dipped any lower the buddha would simply slide forward and shoot over the entrance and into the muddy water. It would go rolling over and over down the steep slope, until it ended up at the bottom of the lake. The thought sent cold shivers through Martin.

There was only one way to prevent that happening – to tie the brass figure so that it would not slip.

Martin looked up and yelled for ropes. He wanted ropes and several men in the water with him to help.

'What will you do, *thakin*?' Po Het demanded, his voice harsh and strained. None of the other *oozies* even moved. They seemed hypnotized by the threatened disaster.

'I am going to lash the buddha to the temple,' Martin yelled, furious at the delay. 'And don't stand staring. Get me some rope . . . and tell some of the men to come into the water. I can't heave the buddha back to a safer position without help.'

Then, as no one moved, he suddenly lost his temper and roared:

'You ... get me some rope,' and he pointed at the nearest *oozie*.

The man stepped back half a pace, and made no other move. Then San Shwe appeared. He had clawed his way up the muddy slope to one of the trees to which the anchor ropes were tied. There had been some yards of spare rope at the foot of one of the trees; this he had cut and now came slithering down the slope in a sitting position and literally tobogganing on the wet ground.

He could easily have shot out into deep water if Martin had not hurriedly splashed forward and checked the youngster's forward rush.

'Thank you,' he said breathlessly when San Shwe had got his balance, and looking up at Po Het he said sarcastically: 'At least someone cares whether the buddha is drowned or not. No one else seems to mind.'

Buoyed up at the back by fourteen oil drums which were doing their best to float it, and held down at the front by the drums Po Het had punctured, the temple would have tipped forward but for the two ropes still securing it to the trees behind. It was actually floating, but if the ropes broke it would swing front down, and then probably sink.

Martin had to get inside, yet he was half afraid that his weight on the front of the temple might prove the 'last straw' which might tip the building just that little bit more and snap the anchoring ropes.

He asked for volunteers from the watching *oozies*. If a few of them came and stood at the front of the temple, and got their hands under the front, they could give enough support to enable Martin to climb in without danger, but his appeal fell on deaf ears. The Burmese were afraid. The temple seemed as if it must surely topple over any moment, and even San Shwe's father called for his son to come out of the water.

Martin was scared, but there was so much at stake that he decided he must try to get inside with only San Shwe checking any downward dip of the front of the temple.

The boy, almost chest deep in water, got his shoulder under the edge of the front of the temple floor and Martin carefully eased himself in, lying half in half out for a moment, in case his weight made the whole structure tilt even more.

'Quick, *thakin*,' San Shwe pleaded. 'I cannot hold it much longer.'

Martin drew a deep breath, then heaved himself forward. The temple dipped, and then bobbed up again. If the ten drums under the front had not been full of water the whole thing would have floated quite nicely. Martin's idea had been a good one, if Po Het had not sabotaged it.

Inside the temple, with the whole thing dipping and bobbing uneasily, Martin took the rope and made a slip knot in one end. The loop he placed over the squat figure of the buddha, easing it down past the middle so there could be no chance of it slipping off.

He pulled the noose tight, then walked towards the back of the temple. The whole thing was so nicely poised that even under his weight the back sank down a few inches. Luckily for Martin the rope was long enough to reach to the back, and he slipped the free end round one of the main supporting timbers, blessing his luck that there was a slight gap between it and the teak boarding.

Outside, now treading water a few yards out from the temple, San Shwe watched, his face a mask of anxiety. His black hair was plastered down to his head, giving him the appearance of a seal.

Martin was breathing heavily, but he was not so frightened now. If he could drag the buddha a few feet back from the door it would shift the weight, and perhaps even bring the temple on to an even keel again. Bracing his feet he wrapped the end of the rope around one hand, then heaved.

Water flew out of the rope under the sudden pressure as the strands tightened, and for a moment Martin thought he had gained an inch or so. When he turned to look at the yellow figure, however, he knew he had not. The buddha was still perched on the very edge of the building.

Four times he tried, even putting one foot against the back of the temple to get the maximum leverage, but without gaining an inch. For all the movement he got the buddha might well have been bolted to the floorboards. It was not only the weight but the cant of the floor. He was trying to drag it uphill.

Then, as he rested for a moment, there came another chorus of panic-stricken cries from the men behind the temple. They were warning him that one of the anchor ropes was breaking.

A strand in one rope had parted, and under the terrific strain it was uncoiling like some tortured snake, while the two remaining strands were pulled thinner and thinner under the extra burden.

'*Thakin . . . thakin*!' San Shwe screamed. 'Come out . . . quick . . . COME OUT!'

Martin was between the devil and the deep blue sea. He stood almost five feet ten, and though he was not yet fully developed, he weighed over ten stones. Standing at the back of the temple he was helping to counteract the tendency of the building to cock up at the rear. If he ran towards the entrance his extra weight at the front might just tip the scales the wrong way.

'*Thakin . . . thakin* . . . get out!' Now the warning cries were coming from all the *oozies*. They could not see Martin, just as he could not see them, but they were no more than a few yards away, separated by the back wall of the temple. 'It is breaking!' That cry came from San Shwe's father, and it spurred Martin to movement.

Five yards separated him from the open air; five yards of down tilted floor, and the temple was bobbing and swaying under his feet. He saw San Shwe paddle to one side, and the youngster's eyes were wide with terror.

Martin started to walk slowly down towards the open air. He felt the temple shudder, as if he was destroying its centre of balance. Suddenly afraid that if he did not hurry he would be too late, he threw caution to the winds and rushed for the open air.

He almost fell, for the temple floor dipped under his feet at his second stride making him lurch wildly. It swung up again, and throwing him completely off balance shot him out into the water in an ungainly flat dive. As he went under with a terrific splash there was a resounding crack from behind the temple as the weakened anchor rope snapped.

Martin did not hear the chorus of dismayed yells, for he was swimming under water afraid that the temple would fall on him. When he surfaced, some twenty yards further on, breathless and shaking, it was to a strange silence. The shouting had died away, and the only sounds he could hear were his own harsh breathing and the thud-thud-thud of his temple pulses.

He turned round to face the temple, and a shiver ran through him. With one anchor rope broken, it was swung round at an angle, held from slipping off the bank into the water by one quivering, over-strained rope.

Treading water for a moment or so while he wiped his hair from his eyes, Martin expected each moment to see the building lunge forward with a tremendous splash, yet it held, pivoted it seemed, on one of the water filled drums which had dug into the wet bank.

San Shwe broke the trance which held him; the young Burmese swam across to ask if he was unhurt. Martin could only nod, and then followed the youngster to the bank, where they were helped out of the water by half a dozen anxious *oozies*.

Po Het stood back, his face masked in a terrific frown. When Martin had wrung some of the water from his shirt the headman came forward, and with the rest of the men and boys crowding round said angrily:

'Now do you see what you have done, *thakin*? Any moment the other rope will snap. Then our temple, and the buddha will be lost in the water. This is your fault. You must open the sluice gate and drain the water away. At once,' he insisted, raising his voice to an angry bellow.

Martin was too shaken to reply. He turned to look again at the temple. It was incredible that it should still remain there, poised it seemed for a dive. The single rope helping to hold it in position was thrumming under the strain. It would not last long. A swing, caused by the water rising even higher, might give that little extra stress needed to snap the rope. If that happened and the temple toppled into the water, then the rope holding the buddha would surely snap. That would be the last link in the chain of disasters; and everything George Blake had said must be guarded against would have taken place. Not only would the temple be gone, but the crowning indignity to the buddha would have been accomplished – he would be thrown headlong down to the mud at the bottom of the drowned valley.

Martin gulped, turned to Po Het and said quietly:

'We will open the sluice gate. Send someone for more ropes to hold the temple until we have drained off the water.'

A gleam of triumph showed in Po Het's eyes for a moment. He nodded, then turned to send men for more rope. He ordered the rest of them out on to the dam top, and as they moved off Martin followed them.

A little muscle was twitching in his right cheek, and his lips were compressed into a thin line. Last night triumph.

This morning disaster. Complete disaster. As he stumbled and slipped on the muddy slope between the trees, he was seeing the final result of it all:

The lake drained; the timber still standing in piles along the course of the shallow river bed – and ruin for his father. Then, as he climbed on to the top of the dam, following the straggling line of *oozies,* a new thought brought fresh hope. If the lake was to be drained, was there any reason why it should not be drained as his father had planned? With the sluice gate opened wide there would be a rush of water, sufficient to float the timber off the banks of the almost dry stream bed. It only needed the *oozies* to be out with their elephants, and the job could be done.

He began to trot, and catching up with Po Het caught the headman by the shirt sleeve.

'Before we let the waters free,' he said hurriedly, 'send the *oozies* out with the elephants, so that when the water is running they can help the teak logs in, and keep them moving. At least we can get part of the timber down river.'

Po Het stopped and there was a bitter smile on his face when he said:

'It is not the young *thakin's* fault that he does not understand. I will explain. The elephants are still out . . . none of the *pajaiks* went for their beasts this morning because one man had brought word of the danger to the temple. It will take more than an hour to collect the elephants. Another hour to get them in position on the banks of the stream. Can you wait two hours?' and he pointed dramatically across the flooded valley to where they could see the temple as it sat slewed out from the bank, one corner half submerged.

Martin stared and was silent. Po Het went on remorselessly:

'You must choose, *thakin* . . . you can save the temple by ordering us to open the sluice gate now, and letting the water go. Or you can send the *pajaiks* out for the elephants. If you save your father's timber you will destroy our temple and our buddha.'

Martin gulped. He chewed on his lower lip for a moment then said huskily:

'Open the sluice gate.'

7

Unexpected hitch

'For a beardless youth, *thakin,* you show great wisdom,' Po Het said, smiling. 'One day you may become as great a man as your father.'

Martin turned away. Though there was nothing in the headman's voice to suggest that he was sneering, the young Britisher had a feeling that somehow he had been tricked. He could not understand why the temple should not have floated. There was sufficient buoyancy at the back to keep that part up, yet the front had been held down as if it had been weighted.

Sick at heart he turned to watch Po Het divide his men into two gangs. The sluice gate was a simple affair, though very effective. George Blake had left a twenty foot gap in his dam, and this he had lined with boulders cemented together to withstand the tremendous rush of water which would pour through when the gate was lifted.

The gate itself, cunningly fashioned from thick teak planking, moved up and down in a slide which was a miracle of native craftsmanship. Using only *dahs* the men had hewn out a channel which was without flaw. When tried out the gate had moved up and down with the same kind of ease one might have expected from something turned out by the finest precision tools.

On each side of the sluice opening, looking much like

something from an old time sailing ship, were two capstans. When the capstans were turned they hauled on chains going down to each side of the sluice gate. The only precaution needed was to see that the teams of men working the capstans kept time.

Martin watched Po Het get his teams in position. He sent eight men across the flimsy bridge which spanned the gap in the dam top. Bars for working the capstan had been lying handy ever since the sluice gates had been closed with the advent of the monsoon.

In minutes the bars had been fitted, the men took a bar each, and waited for the signal. A bright yellow arrow had been painted on the concrete in which the capstans were sunk, indicating which way the men had to push in order to raise the sluice gate.

Po Het yelled. The men bent their knees and begun to push. There was a momentary clink as chain slack was taken up. Then both capstans stopped with a jerk. The men heaved, then looked enquiringly at the headman.

Martin looked at him, and Po Het was startled. He raised both arms above his head and yelled again. Once more the men bent to the work, but if they had been trying to move a mountain they could not have met with less success. Martin put his shoulder to one of the capstan bars, and Po Het added his weight and strength. There was no response.

'We'll have to ease each side in turn,' Martin said. 'Call the other men across here. Perhaps if we can move each chain a little in turn, we can get the sluice open.'

He was growing more and more anxious now about the

temple. The flood of water pouring into the drowned valley from the surrounding hills was lifting the level at a dangerous speed. If the temple was to be saved they would have to get the sluice gate open very quickly, even if only a foot or so.

One by one the *oozies* made their way across the narrow catwalk, and now there were three men to each capstan bar. It was impossible to get more man-power to work, for the bars were not long enough.

Martin gave the order to heave, and eighteen men gave every ounce of strength they had. For a moment it seemed as if even their combined power was to have no effect. Then, and with the movement there came the agonizing scream of tortured metal, the capstan turned an inch or so. It turned, then jammed, and was completely immovable, backwards or forwards.

'That sound?' Martin queried, 'where did it come from. There is something jammed, I'm sure,' and he looked down towards the bottom of the capstan. Po Het looked as mystified as the rest of the men.

Martin moved forward and dropping to one knee at the foot of the capstan lifted a sheet metal cover which gave weather protection to the point where the capstan's bearings went into the concrete.

'Oh!' He closed his eyes in sudden dismay at what he saw. The reason why it had been so hard to move the capstan even an inch or so was obvious at once. Set in the concrete, on either side of the capstan were two iron eyebolts. Through the eyebolts, and through the base of the capstan a steel bar had been pushed. It was a simple but effective 'safety catch', put in, Martin was sure, as a precaution against anyone opening the sluice without authority.

Taking half a dozen men across to the other capstan Martin took out the safety bolt from the base of that, and the six men had no difficulty in turning it for a quarter of a turn. Then that too jammed. The chain was as taut as if the links had all been forged in one piece.

Looking down at the sluice gate Martin could see water shooting out from one corner in a minor flood. What they had done was to lift one side of the gate a few inches, but they had then jammed the gate in its slides. He ordered the men to turn the capstan back, and the gate dropped again.

'What will you do now?' Po Het demanded, and there was a snarl in his voice.

'You can send your fastest runner to the bungalow,' Martin said. 'Tell him to say that I need files and a hacksaw. If we can cut through the bolt on the other capstan, we will be able to open the sluice.'

'If you cannot?'

Martin shrugged.

'If I can get the hacksaws . . . we can,' he said firmly. 'It is just a question whether we can do it in time, that is all.'

Po Het sent one of the men off, then Martin had another thought. He told Po Het to send the *pajaiks* out for the elephants.

'I shall work as quickly as possible to free the capstan,' he said, 'but in the meantime let us be ready to get the logs downriver when the sluice gate is open.'

'We should be thinking about the house of buddha,' Po Het shouted. 'You do not care what happens to it so long as the logs are got out.'

'You take as many men as you like to the temple,' Martin said angrily, 'and you can have what material you like to make the temple safe. Tell me what you want?'

It took the wind out of Po Het's sails, and he stood glaring, scratching at the shin of his right leg with the toes of his left foot, while the *oozies* stood and waited. When it was apparent that the headman was not going to order the *pajaiks* out, Martin turned to San Shwe's father.

'See to it that the *pajaiks* bring in the elephants,' he said. 'It seems to me that there is one man, at least, who does not want my father to succeed. When all this is ended I think the man named Po Het will be in trouble.'

San Shwe's father turned and hurried off, and for the next half-hour there was an uneasy silence among the Burmese standing on the dam top. Martin tried not to keep looking down the valley for the messenger. Every minute seemed to stretch out into ten.

Each time his eyes strayed across the water the temple seemed to be in a more precarious position than before, yet miraculously it remained out of the water. How long it would remain there he could not guess, for the lake level was rising all the time.

Then the messenger came back, carrying two hacksaws and a packet of blades, as well as half a dozen files, a hammer and a cold chisel. George Blake had questioned the messenger, realised what had happened, and had sent just what tools would be useful.

In the next hour Martin broke seven hacksaw blades, knocked the skin off his knuckles, and managed to saw almost a third way through one side of the retaining bolt. It was not that the metal was extradorinarily hard, nor yet that the saws were of poor quality. The trouble was that he could not get the saw to the bolts at a proper angle.

Towards the end of the third hour, when he was feeling completely exhausted, mentally and physically, his last hacksaw blade snapped. There was a sympathetic hissing of indrawn breaths from the watching *oozies* as Martin sat back on his haunches, and wiped the stinging sweat from his eyes. This was the last straw. He had tried everything. He had attacked the eyebolts with the hammer and cold chisel in the hope of breaking them away. Had he been able to do that it would have freed the capstan at once.

Unfortunately the eyebolts were an inch thick in the neck, and when he tried to break them out of the concrete in which they were set he met with no success at all. George Blake had made a thorough job of everything about Thunder Dam. He knew that if he succeeded he would be able to take teak out of the valley for many years to come, and then leave his son Martin to follow him. During all the years that teak had been cut in Burma, none had gone from this valley because of the poor water channel. To float teak out needed a sudden roaring surge of water, the kind of flood which could only come from a dammed-up lake. Martin's father had done his best to ensure that everything he did in the structure of Thunder Dam would last.

So far as Martin was concerned the work was too well done. In this crisis he could not break up anything his father had built. He sat there, holding the useless hacksaw in his right hand while he sucked the skinned knuckles of his left hand. He had never felt so tired and dejected.

Then Po Het stepped forward to ask:

'What is to be done now, *thakin?*' and there was a challenge in his voice. 'The water rises quickly, and very soon the temple will be washed into deep water. We have put more ropes about it, but they will not hold. You *must* let the water run out.'

If anyone had commiserated with him at that moment Martin might easily have cried, he was feeling so completely tired out and defeated. Po Het's words brought on a sudden tearing rage; a moment of lost temper which sent every sensible thought to the four winds.

To be told he had to do something, when for three hours he had struggled to free the jammed capstan, while these brown skinned Burmese had stood by, not one of them offering to help, almost sent him berserk. He leaped to his feet so quickly that not only Po Het, but every man there, hurriedly scuttled back a few yards, and were ready to run for their lives.

It was not often they saw a white person look like this.

'I have *got* to let the water out!' Martin roared. 'What have you done to help? Get out of my sight, the lot of you. And if you are frightened of what is going to happen to your temple I'll tell you now . . . I'll see that nothing happens to it. Go on, get out,' and he advanced towards them.

One man started to run, and his panic was infectious. Even Po Het joined in the retreat, but he stopped when he was half way to the end of the dam and yelled:

'If the temple is lost, *thakin* Blake, there will be no teak ever taken out of this valley.'

Martin was so furious that he bent and picked up the hacksaw, almost in the same way that a man might bend to pick up a stone to throw at a troublesome dog. The action accelerated the retreat, and even the headman caught up with the others in the dash to get out of harm's way.

Nor did they stop running until they were off the dam top and on the narrow track leading to the village. Martin watched them glumly. He saw them divide into little groups as they hurried on, and guessed they were discussing the young *thakin's* madness. He sat down, elbows on knees, his forehead cupped in his aching palms. What a fool he had been. His father had warned him against losing his temper.

He sat staring miserably in front of him, and wishing he could undo the damage he felt sure he had caused. The people of the village were the only ones who could help him, and he had bellowed at them as if they had been children.

What was more he had said something even more silly. He had told them that they had no reason to fear for the safety of their temple. That *he* would see nothing happened to it. Sick at heart at his foolishness he picked up the hacksaw and the collection of broken blades, the hammer and the cold chisel. Tools that had failed him. He had a sudden wild urge to throw them all into the muddy water.

He stood staring across the lake. By contrast with the previous day there had been only one or two showers. They had been short and sharp, then the sun had dispersed the clouds again. The sun was shining now, and the air felt sweet and almost cool.

Strangely enough the temple was still there, though there seemed to be more of it under water. He looked down at the sluice again. It was like having a loaded money box and no key. If he could only open that sluice the day was just right for the task of getting the logs on the move. The elephants were on hand, the *oozies* would get to work – if only the water could be set roaring out of that locked door. If . . . if . . . if!

Slowly, dejectedly, he started to walk along the dam top, and was within thirty yards of the end when he heard a strange sound. It was the music of a stream; water babbling merrily, and quite close at hand. There had been plenty of water sounds in the past thirty-six hours, rain slashing out of the sky and streaming across the ground. This noise, however, was different. It sounded like a pleasant little mountain rill.

He walked to the open valley side of the dam and looked along its long, sloping length. At first he could see nothing unusual. Then he saw a spreading stain on the brown earth banking. It was some forty feet down from where he was standing and a little ahead of him. A sudden suspicion that the dam had sprung a leak made his heart begin to pound a little, and he hurried on to a spot where he could stand and look directly down on the darkening patch of banking.

It was then he realised where the gurgle and chatter of running water came from. Less than eight feet below him water was gushing out of the bank, running down in a channel it had swiftly cut for itself, until meeting much harder earth it was spreading out on the surface, and showing that darker stain.

Dropping the tools he scrambled over the edge of the dam to examine the spot where the water was coming through. It was not possible to look right through to the other side of the embankment, but water was pouring through, and what was worse was washing earth away with it. The hole was widening each moment.

He scrambled back on to the dam top and made to slide over the other side to see if there was a possibility of making a temporary repair job. Only then did he realise how high the water had risen in the past hours. While he had been trying to free the jammed capstan the lake had risen and risen until now it was only some six feet from the top!

He stared down at the smooth surface. There was no wind, there were no waves. The stretch of man-made lake looked as innocent as any boating lake back in Britain, yet if it broke loose it could unleash death and destruction on the village. It could sweep the flimsy huts away, and drown their owners. Yes, and it could overwhelm his father's bungalow.

Martin stared in horror for a few moments while the significance of that small leak got home. His father had said that the level must never get above ten feet from the top of the dam. If his estimation was right, the water was already four feet above the danger mark, and the dam was already showing signs of breaking up.

Dropping the useless tools for the second time he turned and ran. For all he knew water might be flooding into the heart of the dam in a score of places. It would weaken it insidiously, an unseen enemy tearing at the heart of the great wall until the pressure tore out a gap. When that happened a mighty flood would go roaring down the valley, tens of thousands of tons of water, a weight no power on earth could withstand.

Fear of such a disaster added wings to Martin's feet, weary though they were, and it was breathlessness which finally slowed him up. He had to rest, for his lungs felt as if they were being scoured with red hot files. Panting, he dropped to his haunches, head down, looking back towards the dam only when the terrible pain in his chest began to ease a little.

He thought he could see the sun shining on other wet patches on the dam bank, and that brought him to his feet again. He had to get his father to a safer place before the disaster swept him and the bungalow to oblivion. When he did reach the bungalow steps he was so unsteady he sprawled face down on the creaking bamboo slats, and for a moment or so was unable to get up.

8

Win all - or lose all

When Martin staggered into his father's bedroom George
Blake had struggled to a sitting position, and he had grabbed the revolver from under his pillow. He stared beyond
his son, half expecting to see a crowd of Burmese *oozies*
beyond, with drawn *dahs* in their hands.

'It's the dam,' Martin gasped, sinking into a chair, 'the
water is . . . '

'The dam !' his father croaked, and blew out a great sigh
of relief. 'I thought it was something worse. Sit still . . .
keep your head down and don't try to talk.' Then he yelled for the cook, who appeared round the door as if he
had been conjured out of the air. He had seen Martin
coming, and had been waiting for the call. His eyes full
of sympathy, George Blake told the man to make some tea
at once, then turning to Martin said: 'Now, take a deep
breath and hold it as long as you can. It is an old trick
for slowing down the beat of the heart. Bend over and
close your eyes. And in future you must never run like
this. That old joke that "Mad dogs and Englishmen go
out in the noonday sun" may be funny on the music halls,
but out here it is suicide. You never run 'less you've got a
mad elephant at your tail.'

Martin was glad to do as his father ordered, and holding
his breath did help a great deal. His thumping heart

slowed down, and when he sat upright again his lungs had almost ceased to give him pain.

The cook appeared very soon with tea, and not until two cups had been filled and Martin had drunk deep did his father allow him to talk. With a sad little smile he said:

'You know, even if the world is coming to an end, a few minutes don't make any difference. And you can't give a proper tale when you are out of breath and panicking.'

'I wasn't panicking,' Martin protested, hurt at the suggestion. 'It just happens that the dam is filled to overflowing, and I thought you ought to know,' and he recounted in as few words as possible the events of the morning. The mishap with the temple, the jamming of the sluice gate capstan, and finally what seemed to be the last straw – the leak in the dam, with water pouring through and showing every indication of growing worse.

To his dismay his father said nothing. He finished his cup of tea then sat staring into space for so long that Martin finally said:

'Dad, what are we going to do? There must be something . . . and it will have to be done quickly. You said that if the water level got within ten feet of the dam top there was danger . . . well, it's higher than that now. It could be within a foot or so of over-flowing.'

His father nodded, but still said nothing. At last he reached out for a cheroot and after nipping off the end struck a match. Not until he had puffed a few times did he say soberly:

'I'm afraid there isn't a thing you can do, Martin; nothing.'

'What!' Martin wailed. 'What . . . you mean . . . but you said we'd lose everything if we didn't get the logs out. Besides, if the dam breaks everything will go. Even this place. There must be something.'

George Blake tapped the end of his cheroot on the ash tray, though there was not sufficient ash to knock off. He was chewing at his lower lip and his eyes were very bleak. He sighed and shook his head.

'There just isn't anything *you* could do, Martin. Nothing. If I could only walk I might . . . but what's the use of saying that. I *can't* walk.'

'Well, if there is something you could do . . . could I do it instead?' Martin asked desperately. 'Father, don't you realise that . . . '

'I realise only too well,' his father said sharply. 'Don't think I'm happy, sitting here and knowing that everything I've worked for during the past three years, yes, and a life's savings, is going to go down the drain. I realise what is going on . . . and if I could I would do something, but I can't.'

'Yes, but you said you could . . . if you could walk,' Martin insisted. 'Tell me and I'll do it.'

Some of the harshness went from George Blake's face, and he laid a hand on Martin's arm. There was resignation in his voice when he said quietly:

'I know you would, but this is one thing you can't do. Well, I won't let you try. There is only one way of getting the water out, before the dam falls apart, and that is by

blowing up the sluice gates. It is too dangerous . . . well,
for you, anyway.'

Martin stared at his father, and his eyes were tragic. He
gulped several times before he was able to speak. Then he
said:

'Too dangerous for me . . . but not for you! Dad, I'm
not a baby. I'm probably as fit as you. Let me try.'

'No. If anything went wrong – I'd never forgive my-
self,' and for the first time ever, Martin detected the hint
of a break in his father's voice. George Blake was going
through one of the worst periods of his whole life. Everything he had worked for was tottering on the brink of
disaster, and he was helpless, chained to his room by two
broken legs.

Martin tried another tack.

'What about Mother, and Sue? What's going to happen
to them if we go bankrupt? We've got to do something.
We can't just sit here . . . and wait for it happening.'

'You don't know what you are saying, Martin. If you
realised . . . '

'I realise this,' Martin said hotly, 'that if you could walk
you would be doing it. All right . . . you can't walk. I
came out here to be your assistant, so you should let me
have a try. At least I can try, Father. Let me try.'

'I'll tell you what it means,' his father said slowly. 'It
means going up to the foot of the sluice gate, boring holes
in the teak planking . . . sticking gelignite in the holes,
walking as far away as you can, unrolling wire, and then
firing the charges.'

'Well I . . . '

'Let me finish, Martin,' his father said patiently. 'While you are drilling holes there will be the danger that the dam will collapse. I told you that if the water level got within ten feet of the top there was danger. I reckoned ten feet was giving us a foot or two spare . . . but you say it is much higher than that. The dam could go any minute – especially as it is leaking from near the top. That's what you would be facing, Martin. You could die and never know how it happened. We'd never see anything of you again.'

'Is that all?' Martin asked quietly.

His father gave him a sharp look then said angrily:

'Now don't be silly, Martin. It isn't funny. I mean every word I say.'

'I am not being funny, Dad,' and slipping off his chair Martin dropped to one knee by the campbed. 'If you don't let me try, I'll never forgive you. If we don't try, what are we going to say to Mother and Sue? That we just sat here, because you wouldn't let me take your place. Dad . . . you still think of me as a youngster. I am growing up.'

His father sat for a minute, his lips compressed to no more than a line, his eyes staring out through the window, yet seeing nothing. At last he said:

'All right, feel in my trousers' pockets. Get my keys.'

Selecting one of the keys he told Martin to go to the store-shed and unlock a strongly built box near the door. It contained gelignite, fulminite-of-mercury caps, and a roll of wire, plus a firing box – the latter a substitute for a battery. There as a plunger, which, when pressed down, turned a small but efficient motor which would generate sufficient power to fire the explosive charges.

The cook was sent across to the village to ask for San Shwe, and was also asked to tell Po Het that there was a danger the dam might burst. He was to evacuate the village, and get as much furniture and rice stores out of harm's way as possible.

When the cook had gone George Blake fitted a dozen sticks of gelignite with the fulminite-of-mercury caps. He showed Martin how to connect them with the firing wires, then explained how he must drill holes in the teak planking of the sluice gate, push the charges in, and when he had got a dozen in place, unreel the wire as far as possible before firing.

'I don't know how much wire there is on the roll,' George Blake explained, 'but try and get on to higher ground if you can. When the sluice gate is blown there'll be a rush of water that could devastate the valley. How strong it will be I don't know, because Thunder Dam has never been in action before.'

'And what about you?' Martin asked, as he packed the equipment into a canvas bag.

'The cook is as loyal a Burmese as you could wish to have,' was the quiet reply. 'He'll stand by me. I'll perhaps get him to call a few men to carry me to a safer spot. Martin, I've said all I mean to say about the danger. If San Shwe does join you – keep him outside the sluiceway, so that he can watch the dam face. If water starts coming over the top . . . I mean actually over the top, then drop the whole business and run for your life. Promise!'

'I promise.' He took his father's outstretched hand.

'If it comes off,' and now his father somehow managed a little smile, 'I'll take you into partnership. Blake and Son, teak exporters.'

Martin tried to smile, but it was a weak effort, no more than a slight quiver of the lips. For a second he had the horrible feeling that he was seeing his father for the last time, and he had a sudden urge to drop the whole idea and stay in the bungalow.

Instead he picked up the bag of explosives, the heavy brace, and the three one-inch steel bits. With their aid, if he was lucky, he might be able to save Thunder Dam from bursting wide open, and destroying everything in the valley. If he was not lucky . . . he experienced a cold shiver, and tried not to think of what would happen if he failed.

The sun was like a ball of polished brass in a sky which was only the palest blue; indication that the monsoon truce would be broken again within the next few hours. It was hot, and the wet ground was already drying up, though not with the iron hardness of the pre-rains.

Looking across the valley he could see men, women and children moving up to the shelter of the trees. They were all carrying things, evacuating their little huts as a precaution against the big dam bursting. There was no sign of the cook returning, and Martin wondered for a moment whether his father's faith in the man was justified.

Pushing his fears to the back of his mind he hurried up towards the dam. It was shiny in places where the sun was glinting on the stream of water coming down the slope. There were more of them now, indication that the water level of the lake was even higher, and was finding more weak spots near the top of the dam itself.

He tried to ignore the splash of water, and the fact that with the leakage, what had been an almost dry stream bed was now a merrily babbling brook. The high concrete walls of the sluiceway seemed to tower up on each side of him like the walls of a skyscraper as he walked into the twenty-four feet wide passage, and up to the teak sluice gate itself.

Thin jets of water, under high pressure, were hissing out from a dozen points, for not even the finest native workmanship could make a wooden gate completely watertight. The air was filled with a fine mist which settled on Martin's eyebrows and eyelashes and he realised again how thorough his father was in everything he did. He had insisted on wrapping the sticks of gelignite in waxed paper, and the box with the tiny dynamo in similar fashion.

'Yes, he knows his stuff,' he murmured as he laid down his bag and got out the big brace and one of the steel bits. The brown teak planking was shiny with water flowing down, but not until he began to bore did he really understand the nature of the job he had taken on.

The bit was new, and the steel made in Sheffield. The cutting edge was first class, but he was trying to bore into one of the world's hardest timbers, and the teak did not cut easily.

It took a muscle-torturing ten minutes to drill the first hole, and he was blowing hard when he put the brace down and inserted the first charge of gelignite. He looked at his watch and pulled a wry face. Just twelve minutes to bore the hole, push the charge in and connect up the wire. If he drilled twelve holes it would be at least two and a half hours before he was ready to blow the sluice gate down.

Even as he rammed the point of the bit against the next plank and started turning the brace he knew he would never do it. Two and a half hours was more time than he could hope for. He pressed even harder against the smooth rounded end of the brace and tried to turn even quicker.

Sweat trickled down into his eyes, his arm muscles began to feel wooden, and he had to keep changing the spot where he was pressing against the brace. His breast bone felt as if someone had hit him with a hammer, yet unless he pressed hard the bit would not cut into the teak.

He had just tamped home the second charge when San Shwe arrived. The young Burmese was excited, and pointing down the valley raised his voice against the hiss of escaping water to shout:

'There is a small aeroplane circling over the fields lower down, *thakin*. Do you think it is the doctor?'

Martin stopped, his eyes lighting up.

'The doctor! Yes, of course. It has been fine most of the day. I expect it is. I think . . . ' and there he stopped. He had been going to say that he would go down to meet the plane, and see what the doctor had to say. He changed his mind almost as soon as the thought occurred to him. There was a more important job to be done.

San Shwe had been sent up by the cook, and taking the brace and bit he bored the third hole, giving Martin a chance to rub his aching arm muscles and get back his breath. He took over for the fourth hole. San Shwe bored the fifth, and while he was doing that Martin walked out of the sluiceway to take a look at the dam. He was astonished to see a big tusker standing a dozen yards away, swaying gently from side to side, his legs shackled with heavy chains.

It was so unexpected that he even forgot to check up on the water flowing down the dam, but hurried back to ask why San Shwe had brought the tusker.

'Po Sun (Mr Firefly) is my father's tusker,' San Shwe explained, 'and my father said I must bring it, for Po Sun is a good swimmer.'

'A good swimmer . . . oh, I see,' and Martin took over the brace and bit. It seemed that San Shwe's father was pessimistic about the dam, and wanted his son to have a chance if Thunder Dam burst.

Doggedly, though he was working more slowly now, Martin drilled the sixth hole. He knew now, for certain, that he would never be able to put twelve charges of gelignite into the sluice gate. Even if he had time, his arm muscles would not stand up to the task.

The bit was grinding more slowly, and the chips of purple-brown wood were thinner and thinner. The will to succeed was there, but the power was fading. Martin was almost drugged with fatigue. He leaned against the brace and wrenched the handle round in a series of spasmodic jerks.

He was just withdrawing the bit from the hole when San Shwe, who had been out to make sure his elephant was all right, came rushing back. His eyes were blazing with excitement and as he grabbed Martin by the arm he screamed:

'*Thakin* . . . *thakin,* we must go. Water is now spilling over the top, all along the dam. We must go now . . . or we shall be drowned. *THAKIN* . . . do you not understand? The water is flowing over the top – all along the top of the dam.'

'You go,' Martin said dully. With fingers which fumbled he was connecting the thin copper wire to the last of the six charges. He was just finishing that when what he thought at first was heavy rain began to fall on him. He hunched his shoulders against it. Then, as San Shwe screamed at him once more, he looked up. Immediately he was half blinded by falling water, and when he shielded his eyes he saw that it was not rain. The water was overflowing from the lake down the sluice opening.

San Shwe was screaming to him to come, and for a moment panic clutched him. He ran almost to the end of the sluiceway, then stopped. He saw the young Burmese race up to the elephant, yelling 'Hmit . . . Hmit . . . Hmit' (sit down). But even before Po Sun had lowered himself San Shwe was scrambling onto his neck. He seemed to take wings in a fear-spurred leap which made light of the distance he had to cover.

Martin was torn for a moment by two desires: one to get away while there was time; the other to make what use he could of the work he had already done. His father had said he could not do it. That thought flashed through his mind and weighed the scales. Frightened though he was, he turned back.

Picking up the roll of wire and the firing box, he began to retrace his steps to the open. San Shwe was having difficulty with Po Sun. The tusker seemed to know that there was growing danger, and he was anxious to get away, yet he dropped to his knees once more as San Shwe rubbed a hard foot behind the elephant's right ear, yelling 'Hmit' as loudly as he could.

'*Thakin . . . thakin*!' San Shwe yelled as Martin came out into the open, and he leaned down, his left arm outstretched, offering a helping hand. Martin shook his head and trotted past the elephant, unwinding the thin wire from the reel, and looking for the best place where he could fire the explosives and still be safe if the dam burst.

He had over a hundred yards to go before the ground began to rise even the slightest, and as he ran Po Sun lumbered to his feet and turned to follow him. San Shwe was almost in tears. He could see what was happening. The whole length of the dam was now like a gigantic overflow, with water streaming down, and flashing white in the sun where it struck stones and was thrown up in spray.

San Shwe kept his anxious elephant walking a few yards behind Martin, and he halted the big tusker when, the wire having run out, the young Britisher laid his firing box on the ground, took the twin ends of copper and plugged them in where his father had shown him they must go.

'*Thakin*, we are here, ready when you are,' San Shwe gasped, bending down so that Martin could not possibly miss what was being said. Martin nodded. For the moment he was not in the same world as the young Burmese. There

was a sluice gate to be blown, a dam to be saved. If he could save Thunder Dam, then there was a chance that he could save his father's work – save them both from ruin.

He knelt over the box, and laid his hands on the plunger. A quick hard press down should send a boosted electric current through to the fulminite-of-mercury caps on the sticks of gelignite. If everything had been done right there would then be a tearing explosion which would rip the teak sluice gate apart.

Drawing a deep breath, and biting his lower lip, he jammed the plunger down in a swift, powerful movement. Almost in the same instant, it seemed, there was a muffled roar from the direction of the sluice. For one frightening second he thought the dam itself must have burst. The sound of the explosion was not quite how he had expected it to be. He had thought there would be a thunderous roar.

As he lifted his head to look towards the sluice he saw dirty brown-yellow smoke rising up from the sluiceway. By contrast to the height and the length of the dam it looked almost insignificant. He waited. Now there must come a great flood of muddy water, perhaps carrying the shattered teak gate on its crest.

The hills had taken up the sound of the explosion, echoing and re-echoing the sound as it was tossed from one side of the valley to the other and back again. But there was no roaring bellow of flood water tearing free. Water still splashed gently over the top of the dam, and ran in glistening silver streams down to the bottom . . . and that was all.

'What is the matter, *thakin?*' San Shwe asked, and

when Martin neither answered nor looked round the young Burmese slipped off the elephant's neck and came across to lay a hand on the young Britisher's arm. In a shocked voice he said: 'It has not worked!'

'That's it,' Martin said heavily. 'It has not worked.' He turned, choking with numbed disappointment. He had done everything he could, taken the frightful risk, and it had been a failure. Dejectedly he began to walk away, making for the bungalow.

He had gone almost a hundred yards when something touched him lightly on the shoulder. He looked round and instinctively cringed away when he realised that it was the tip of Po Sun's trunk. The big tusker had come up quietly behind him, San Shwe riding on his neck, and was now gently moving him out of the way.

'Will you ride, *thakin*?' the young Burmese called. 'It is . . . ' and the rest of his words were drowned by a reverberating roar which seemed to fill the valley with an awe-inspiring bellow. It was like a thunderbolt, only different. Almost as if something had suddenly been released. Martin started to turn, then stopped, and closed his eyes. He knew what it was. The worst had happened after all his efforts: the dam had burst. Thunder Dam had gone!

9

The temple and buddha are lost!

'*Thakin!*'

The scream from San Shwe made Martin look up, but the slim brown arm was pointing back up the valley, and it was not woe or fright that weighted the voice of the youngster; it was a mixture of disbelief and joy.

Martin dodged to one side and looked past the big grey elephant. He expected to see the whole of the dam crumbling away, water pouring in a frightening flood into the valley below, with perhaps the concrete of the sluiceway standing above it all.

The picture was different. Water *was* flooding into the valley, but it was coming from the sluiceway in what looked like a solid box of water. It was five yards square, and keeping its shape for many yards, just as a jet of water from a hose pipe will if there is sufficient power behind it. There was immense power behind this solid mass of water; the whole weight of the artificial lake penned up by Thunder Dam. It was all pressing to escape through the wide open sluice.

Martin saw, for a few seconds, the shattered teak planking which had formed the sluice gate. Broken pieces were being tossed about on the foaming crest of the flood like dark little match sticks. He saw them for a second or so, then they were engulfed and not seen again.

It seemed too good to be true; yet the explanation was simple enough. The six charges of gelignite had not been powerful enough to shatter the teak gate, but they had weakened it. The tremendous pressure of water had started the planks to bulge. They had bulged more and more then finally split open, with the ensuing crash which had sounded so like thunder.

Martin stood and stared, though after the first twenty seconds he was not actually seeing the brown flood as it roared down the valley, filling the river bed and catching up the stacked teak as if they were no more than chips of soft timber. He was swallowing a lump in his throat, and blinking rapidly in an effort to keep back tears of joy and relief.

It was left to San Shwe to break the trance which held Martin in its grip. The young Burmese had been throwing his arms into the air from sheer joy until he saw that the young white *thakin* was apparently quite unimpressed. It sobered the young Burmese and he shook his head in puzzled bewilderment.

There had been so much risk, so much danger, that he had expected Martin to go mad with joy when, after apparent failure, his efforts had succeeded. He could not realise that Martin Blake was so near to tears that he dare not move or say anything.

'*Thakin*, would you not like to see the elephants working the timber? See, the *oozies* are taking them down river.' San Shwe pointed down the valley where a line of elephants were making their way to the water, the

brightly coloured shirts and tucked-up *lungyis* (skirts) of the men showing up clearly against the dark grey of the tuskers' hides.

Po Sun slid to his knees at a command, then San Shwe helped Martin up on to the thick neck. In that moment of relief Martin would have agreed to almost any suggestion. He was suffering from shock; dazed with the hours of mental tension and physical labour. He was like a long distance runner who has used up all his power and, having won the race, has strength for nothing for some time afterwards.

The next ninety minutes passed like a dream, but an exciting dream, and it helped Martin get over the agony that had gone before. Sitting with San Shwe on the back of Po Sun he watched eleven *oozies* and their elephants keeping the timber on the move.

The brown flood having reached the stacked timber, burst in explosions of foam and threw logs weighing two, three and even four tons into the air. Some went swiftly with the current, others dropped awkwardly after the first mighty rush, and jamming in the river bed started other logs piling up behind them.

Martin thought he had never seen anything so dangerous, so exciting, or so courageous as the work of the elephants and their *oozies*. The tuskers waded into the flood until the water was lapping the drawn up legs of their *oozies*. Squealing and trumpeting they attacked the log jams, easing out one big trunk of teak after another, and finally tossing the key log free.

Time after time it seemed certain that someone would be killed, for the mighty teak butts were racing down river like light canoes shooting rapids. Yet the tuskers seemed to move by instinct. They would whirl round to take a glancing blow on the buttocks, then roar, half in pain, half in triumph, as the log moved off into deep water and was whirled away. It was an exhilarating battle; an exciting contest of animals and men versus logs and the river.

Sunset ended the trial of strength and by that time the elephants were several miles down stream, and the flood was beginning to flatten out a little. The sky turned pink, deepening to purple, and almost in an instant it seemed the stars were shining.

Above the thrum and hiss of the river Martin could hear the *oozies* yelling to one another as they turned homewards, and he suddenly realised that since the sluice gate burst he had never given a thought to his father.

Po Sun ambled along, seeming slow enough in his gait, yet making a good four miles an hour, and when the last of the day had gone from the western sky Martin slipped off the tusker's neck and walked towards the bungalow. Not until then did he realise how stiff and sore he was.

His chest ached as if it had been hammered, and his arm muscles felt as if they were held in a vice. Yet he had never been quite so ridiculously happy before. They had won. The odds had looked unsurmountable. His father had felt they had lost the battle . . . and he, Martin Blake, had won his spurs. He had proved that he was a man, even if he was still only in his teens.

Only as he mounted the veranda steps did it strike him that there was only a very small light in his father's room. Then he remembered the light plane which San Shwe reported earlier circling over the paddy field landing field.

He stepped off the veranda, thinking that perhaps the doctor had done something and then given his father a sleeping-draught. He walked across to the cooking shelter where he could see Maung Tha busy over his pans.

'What happened this afternoon?' he asked. 'Is my father asleep? He . . . Oh!' The exclamation was jerked out of him by sight of Po Het. The village headman was squatting on his haunches in one corner of the cooking hut, a plate of rice in his left hand, a ball of rice in the fingers of his right hand.

The cook's eyes flickered uneasily as if he had unexpectedly been caught doing something wrong.

'Po Het is here to speak to you, *thakin*,' he said. 'Because you were so late I offered him rice.'

'That is right,' Martin said. 'Now I asked you about my father. Does he sleep? Has the doctor been?'

'*Thakin* Blake has gone in the plane with the doctor to Akyab,' Maung Tha said soberly. 'There is a message on the table in *thakin* Blake's room.'

'Thank you.' Martin turned and hurried across to the bungalow, vaguely aware of the elephant Po Sun kneeling a few yards away, and the figure of San Shwe by its head.

On to the veranda in a single bound, across to the table where he turned up the lamp, then picked up the single sheet of paper held from blowing away by the ash tray. It took no more than a few moments to read the short note.

Martin, I am going to Akyab hospital for a few days, and will be back just as soon as there is another good flying day. I hope the sluice job was successful. If not, do not worry too much. I have taken plenty of hard knocks over the years, and with you to help me we will get over this trouble. The doctor says he thinks my legs will soon be all right, but he wants to see them under X-ray before he does anything. Keep your chin up. Dad.

Martin closed his eyes and grinned. It was going to be a wonderful moment when his father did come back. There might be a good many logs not floating down to the main river, but he had saved the dam, and much of the teak would get down to the wharves. They would not go 'broke'.

'*Thakin*!' He turned with a start, not having heard Po Het enter the room. In the light of the oil lamp, for the pressure lamp was still to be lit, the headman looked to Martin more villainous than ever.

'What is it?' he asked, finding it difficult to be polite. They had parted on the top of the dam some hours before, and then Po Het had been running after Martin's angry, and rather despairing, outburst. In the excitement of the past hours Martin had completely forgotten the temple and the buddha; but it all came back to him now with sickening force.

The temple had been half in, half out of the water, held by one or two ropes. The attempt to open the sluice gate and lower the level of the lake had been a desperate last

minute attempt to save the temple. As he looked at Po
Het, Martin had a premonition that the inevitable had
happened – the ropes had parted and the temple had fallen
into the lake. His fears were confirmed within seconds, for
Po Het said:

'This afternoon, *thakin*, with the *oozies* there to bear
witness, you gave us a promise that no harm would come
to our temple and the buddha. That is true, is it not?'

'It is true,' Martin agreed, and his throat felt dry and
his heart was thumping.

'*Thakin*, there is no temple now, there is no buddha,'
Po Het said coldly. 'You let the water in the lake rise and
rise until you had enough to float down the teak, and as a
result . . .'

'That is a lie,' Martin burst in angrily. 'You know very
well I did all I could to open the sluice and let the
water . . .'

'*Thakin*,' Po Het said heavily, 'it is in the writing between your father and the Government that no harm shall
come to our temple or buddha. When the new day comes
you will see that they are both gone – swallowed up by the
lake. There will be trouble when my people know of this.'

'But it wasn't my fault,' Martin pleaded. 'If the sluice
gate capstans hadn't . . .'

Po Het silenced him with an imperious wave of one
hand. In that moment he looked, and behaved, as if he
was completely master of the situation. Coldly, yet calmly
he said:

'*Thakin*, you are a young man, and only a cruel man
would put too much blame on a beardless youth. I am

sorry for you, and if you will take an older man's advice you will pack your things as quickly as you can. I will call San Shwe to bring his elephant, and before morning you can be on your way to join your father in Akyab. If you stay here, evil may be done to you. My people will be very angry.' He stood for a moment, staring at Martin, then gave him a little salutation, turned on his heels, and went out.

The showdown

The cook came quietly into the room and laid the table for the evening meal. He told Martin that his bath was ready, and like an automaton the young Britisher went into his own room, bathed and changed. He was like someone in a trance. It seemed wrong, criminally wrong that he should have fought so hard, and been so near victory only to be defeated at the very last moment.

'And it is defeat,' he whispered as he sat down before the plate of soup the soft voiced cook had brought in. 'We'll never live this down. The temple and the buddha were the key points in the concession. The people had to be kept happy, and that meant keeping the buddha in his place.'

He ate the meal mechanically, and was drinking his second cup of coffee when there was an urgent whisper from the doorway:

'*Thakin* . . . may I come in. I have news for you.'

Martin half turned. In the stress of the past hour he had completely forgotten San Shwe, and gave a little groan as he realised how badly he had treated the young Burmese. San Shwe had stood by him during the dangerous two hours when he had been putting the explosive charges in the sluice gate, and he deserved better than to have been left waiting outside.

'I'm terribly sorry, San Shwe,' he said, rising. 'I have had bad news, and that made me . . .'

'Bad news, *thakin*?' San Shwe whispered, and added, 'about the buddha?'

'Yes, Po Het has told me that the temple has gone, and the buddha with it. Gone into the lake, and probably smashed to bits against the sides of the sluiceway when the current took it down there.'

'No, *thakin*, no,' San Shwe said hurriedly. 'That is why I am here now. I have been back to my home for fodder for Po Sun. I did not want to send him off to find his own food for this side of the valley can be dangerous. I have just crossed the top of Thunder Dam, carrying food for the elephant, and there is a moon. By its white light I saw the buddha.' His voice sank to a whisper as he added urgently, '*Thakin*, you must move the buddha, for he lies face down in the mud. If our people see him like that there will be trouble – they will blame you and your father.'

Martin was moving towards the door almost before San Shwe had finished speaking. He collected his big electric torch, and was starting for the dam when he had a thought. The buddha was far too heavy for the two of them to move. Lips pursed he pondered for a moment whether he could trust Maung Tha to help him.

His father had complete faith in the cook, who had been in his service for many years. He turned towards the kitchen, and watching Maung Tha's face by the light of the oil lamp, gave the news San Shwe had just brought.

'I must move the buddha,' he said quietly. 'You are my father's man. Will you help me?'

Maung Tha's face remained expressionless for a few moments, then he said soberly:

'For twelve years your father has been father and mother to me. I have never gone to him for help and been refused. Has this boy got his elephant with him?'

San Shwe had just given Po Sun the fodder he had brought, and the big tusker, tethered on the valley side of the bungalow, grumbled and protested at being mounted again when he thought he had finished for the day.

They collected ropes from the store shed, and two extra oil lamps; these would only be lit when they got down into the mud-covered valley bottom. Down there the wall of the dam would prevent any lights being seen from the village, and secrecy was vital.

The moon kept disappearing behind occasional patches of cloud, but when it was clear it lit up the scene, and made walking fairly easy. They crossed the top of Thunder Dam, and the elephant's big feet squelched noisily in the mud. It seemed impossible that only a few hours earlier water had been pouring over the top of the dam. Now there was no lake, and only a big expanse of moonlit mud remained, with a stream running down the centre.

It was an eerie scene, more eerie still when they came to the centre where water flowing into the valley from the hills was draining down through the wide open sluice gate. Here the buddha was lying half buried in the mud, his smiling face hidden from view.

The temple was some eight yards away, also face down. Martin walked past the buddha to see what damage had been done to the building. At the back of his mind was a half formed idea that he might be able to get the elephant to drag the temple away. They had the whole night ahead of them, and if the temple could be salvaged and the buddha put in his place again, washed and polished, they might yet win.

The oil drums were still securely lashed under the temple, and it was when he laid a hand on one of them that he felt the dent, and then the gash. Switching on his torch he examined every drum, and in place of the desperation he had felt earlier there was now a growing rage.

He called Maung Tha and San Shwe, pointing out how someone had sabotaged the drums, and explaining to them how with water in the ten split drums the temple was bound to sink.

'And don't try and tell me that this was the work of jungle *nats*,' he stormed. 'This is the work of a man . . . or men. San Shwe . . . you live in the village, surely you must have an idea who is behind this.'

'No, *thakin,* no. No idea,' the young Burmese protested. 'If I knew I would tell, for to you my father owes his life.'

'All right, we are going to turn the temple right way up,' Martin said dourly. 'We'll wash it clean, put the buddha back, after we've given him a wash, then haul them out to dry land. I'll show whoever did this to us that they can't get away with it.'

While the big tusker pulled the overturned temple back onto the oil-drum raft Maung Tha climbed the steep face of the dam and hurried back to the bungalow for a bucket and cloths. When he returned he helped Martin and San Shwe to get the buddha back in his place in the temple.

Then they began the big clean-up. They carried buckets of water from the stream flowing nearby. They sluiced the water over the outside and the inside of the temple, until they were sure that everything was as clean as it could possibly be.

San Shwe washed the buddha, and dried the brass figure lovingly. Then they harnessed Po Sun to the temple again, and to a chorus of 'Yoo . . . yoo . . . yooo' (pull – pull – pull) the mighty tusker leaned into the harness and tried to drag the temple away from the middle of the sea of mud. Though his feet were like huge dinner plates, and though he used his great strength with all the intelligence of an animal brought up to hauling heavy teak logs, Po Sun could not defeat the mud. He could not get a solid foothold, and slithered this way and that and sent mud flying all over the place, and finally, realising he could not move the temple, he ceased trying.

'It is no use, *thakin*,' San Shwe said resignedly. 'When an elephant knows he cannot do a task he stops, and it is useless to try to make him start again.'

Martin fumed and fretted. He knew that even though they had put the temple right side up, and cleaned off the mud, it was not enough to convince the villagers of anything other than the fact that buddha could look after himself. The blame for him sitting there at the bottom of what had been the lake would rest fairly and squarely on the shoulders of Martin and his father.

'Is there no way of finding out who is trying to get us thrown out?' he demanded. 'Surely you must have some idea who is fighting against us,' and he looked from San

Shwe to the older Maung Tha. Both Burmese shook a
denial. Then Maung Tha laid a hand on Martin's arm and
whispered.

'*Thakin*, not long after I became your father's cook, he
had to discover who of fifty men had committed a murder.
Many knew who the murderer was, but he was a fierce
man, and so no one would give the murderer's name. Your
father had a way and maybe if we try the same thing it
will show us who is working against us,' and lowering his
voice so that San Shwe would get no details, Maung Tha
explained how Martin's father had brought to book a murderer. It was a slim chance, but better than nothing and
Martin decided to try this last throw of the dice.

*

Half an hour after dawn the entire village gathered in the
mud of what had been the lake. The skies were heavy with
cloud again, promising more torrential downpours before
the day ended. Men and women, and even the children
were solemn faced, for they were here to be told which
among them had tumbled the temple and their buddha
into the lake.

Martin leaned one hand against the side of the temple
and addressed the crowd. He had rehearsed what he had
to say a score of times during the night, and was heavy-
eyed, for he had not slept at all.

'The evening after we placed the oil drums under the
temple, someone came out from the village when all were
asleep. He carried a *dah*, and with it he slashed at ten of
the oil drums. Then, when the lake waters rose the drums

filled, and instead of helping the temple to float, they tried
to drag it under.'

Men and women looked hastily round at their neighbours, but no one spoke. Martin went on:

'In this box,' indicating a packing-case standing nearby,
'there is white man's *truth seeker*. I want every man in
turn to step forward, put his hand through the slit in the
curtain which is across the front of the box. Inside the box
he will find something which feels like a rope. He must
squeeze it. If he is innocent, nothing will happen, but the
guilty one will be made known to you all.'

He looked sharply round the crowd, the men looked
down uneasily, the women clutched at their babies. Then
Martin went to the front of the box, put his hand in, and
after a moment or so withdrew it. Maung Tha followed
Martin's example, and after him San Shwe, and San
Shwe's father. Reluctantly at first, but with less fear when
nothing happened, the *oozies* followed suit.

Tension built up as the number of men and boys still to
be 'tried' grew less and the mysterious 'trial' box had still
given no outward sign. Finally only two men were left,
an old man and Po Het. His face grey with fright the old
man shuffled up and thrust a trembling hand into the box.
His arm muscles twitched as he squeezed the mysterious
thing inside the box, then he brought out his hand and
gave a sigh of relief.

There was an almost paralysing nervous strain among
the crowd when the headman walked up. There was a
film of sweat on his forehead, but his eyes were defiant and
there was a sneer on his face as he thrust his hand into the

box, held it there for a few moments and then withdrew it. And nothing happened!

'So,' Po Het sneered. 'No one slashed the oil drums. It seems that it was the jungle *nats* who did this to show . . . '

'Wait,' Martin said calmly. 'There is one final part of this trial to come. Now every man must pass his right hand close to my face. The hand he thrust into the box.'

'This is madness,' Po Het protested. 'Why should . . . '

'If you are innocent there is nothing to fear,' Martin said curtly. 'Come . . . begin.'

The procession marched slowly in front of Martin, each man and boy thrusting his open hand within inches of the young Britisher's face, and still there was no sign from the box. Then came the last of them all; once more Po Het was sneering as he thrust his hand almost into Martin's face. He held it there and laughed when nothing happened. Then, as he turned to walk away, a queer, chanting voice from within the temple broke the nerve-wracked silence:

'He is the one who smashed the oil drums and helped throw me into the lake. If he tells the truth now I will show mercy to him. If he will not tell the truth then I will avenge the terrible thing he has done. I have spoken.'

There was a whispering hiss of indrawn breaths, then silence. All eyes were on Po Het. The villagers stared at him as if sure that any moment now he would be struck dead.

The headman, already turning away from Martin, stopped as if he had been turned to stone. His mouth open, his eyes widened in terror, he slowly turned to look into the

temple where the buddha squatted in the gloom. No one spoke. Even the babies in their mothers' arms were quiet. The scene was wrapped in a breathless, frightening silence.

Then Po Het's knees began to shake. Slowly he sank down and bowed his forehead into the mud. Then, still in that frightening silence, he shuffled forward on his knees until he could lay his forehead on the front of the temple floor. He broke the silence, and there was an agony of fear and remorse in his croaking words as he whispered:

'Forgive me . . . forgive me. It was not all my fault. One came to me with a present of opium, and I was a fool to take it. Then I wanted more opium, and this powerful one gave me more opium. I had more and more from him . . . until I could not live without it.'

There were hissing intakes of breath at this, for the Government was trying hard to stamp out the curse of opium eating.

'Then,' Po Het continued, 'he came to say that I must stop *thakin* Blake from getting the teak out. He told me to remove the sacred buddha from the temple, and four men who have hidden in the jungle came to help me. He told me other things I had to do . . . promising me money and more opium if I did as he asked, and terrible punishment if I did not. Forgive me!' and he dropped his head again.

The crowd stared at him, horrified and seemingly paralysed at his confession.

'Tell them to go back to their homes, Maung Tha,'

Martin whispered. 'The *oozies* must bring their elephants, and we will have the temple dragged out of here, and placed in the village.'

Maung Tha gave the orders, and the villagers did not need a second telling. They turned, hurrying away in a frightened silence. Then Martin took hold of Po Het's arm and helped the shaking headman to his feet.

'There could be great punishment for this thing,' he said sternly. 'In a few days my father will return. Until then . . . you will stay in your hut.'

'Yes, *thakin,* yes,' Po Het had lost all his bombast, and he bowed again to the silent buddha, then walked away, head bowed and shoulders shaking. Martin looked at Maung Tha, then wiped the beads of perspiration which dewed his own brow and upper lip.

'That was well done,' the cook said admiringly. 'Your father never had a "voice" to help him. But then he was more experienced than you.'

'Well, we'll get the tape recorder back into the bungalow as soon as everyone is out of sight,' Martin said, beginning to detach the little switch he had fixed on to the side of the temple, and against which he had kept his hand throughout the whole proceedings. 'I wouldn't like them to discover that it wasn't their buddha who broke Po Het's nerve.'

*

Later that morning, with twelve big tuskers roped to the temple the building was dragged easily through the mud, up the sloping side of the valley, and then across the end of Thunder Dam, and down to the village. When that was done the *oozies* were ordered to take their elephants along the river, to get any logs which were left down by the water's edge, to clear any log jams, and tidy things up for when George Blake came back from Akyab.

That night, in clean khakis, with the pressure lamp hissing above his head, Martin sat down to write his first letter home. He mentioned that his father had gone to Akyab for a few days, but did not say anything about the broken legs. But he did tell his mother and sister how he had defeated Po Het, and uncovered the reason for the mysterious things that had happened to the temple and the buddha.

'It was Father's cook who tipped me off to a trick Father had used once before. I got all the villagers lined up, and the men had to stick one hand into the front of a packing case. I had a bit of curtaining across the front so they could not see what was inside. They had to grasp the thing hanging inside the box. It was just a piece of fuzzed-out rope soaked in some of that anti-mosquito cream I brought out with me. If you remember the stuff has the most awful smell.

'I said that the rogue would be unmasked by this "magic". Nothing happened, of course. Then I ordered everyone to come up and pass his hand in front of my face. I was banking on the guilty person, or persons, being afraid to grab the rope. And luckily for me the people here really believe in *nats* (jungle spirits to you) so they were convinced the rogue would be unmasked. The real trouble-maker was the headman, a chap named Po Het. He was crafty enough not to squeeze the rope I had hung inside the box, and that gave him away, because when I checked on the hands his did not smell of mosquito cream.

'I had spent half the night fixing up Dad's tape recorder behind the buddha, and I had recorded a few words which I hoped would scare the guilty rascal into confessing. They were all nervous, but I was in a blue funk, in case it didn't work. I hope I never have to go through an experience like it again. It worked, but if it had failed I don't know what I would have done.

'I have made two good friends here. Dad's cook, a splendid chap named Maung Tha, and a lad about my age named San Shwe – he is a *pajaik* (he hooks the elephant chains to the logs) and when Dad comes back I am going to ask him to give them a special present for their loyalty. They were both absolutely splendid. But for them things could have been disastrous.

'I suppose Dad will have written you from Akyab. I am expecting him back in a day or so, and if he hasn't written I'll give him a nudge. We shall be pretty busy for some time to come as the sluice gate of Thunder Dam is gone to glory, and we'll have to make another. I think that is about all. I am going to enjoy the work out here. Love to you both, and remember me to everybody at home.

Your apprentice *Teak Wallah,* Martin.'

Three days later Martin's father was flown back from Akyab, and he dealt with Po Het. Then the craftsmen were set to work to make a new sluice gate. Until that was in place no more water could be built up behind Thunder Dam, but Blake and Son, Teak Exporters, were reasonably happy, for sufficient teak had been floated down to the main river to see them over until the next monsoon season when there would be no more trouble over the temple and its buddha.